After settling d
Colton Lyon ju:
behind him, but
had come back to bite him in the ass. Now
he's found himself hooked up with a mixed
bag of bikers and military types, whose
mission is to take down a group of high
profile parasites, who're into everything
from human trafficking to who knows what.

On top of that he's got a fifteen year old
daughter, the apple of his eye, who thinks
she's in love, and a five year old who's
gonna be featured on America's Most
Wanted before she's fifteen, if he doesn't
keep an eye on her. And then there's his
mother and his wife, the Xmas freaks, who
would raise all kinds of hell if the season
doesn't go off without a hitch.

So between watching his six, trying to hold
himself back from killing the little snot nose
kid who's been sniffing around his first
born, he's got to make sure his wife's
holiday season is all that is merry and bright.

Lyon's Xmas Special
Jordan Silver

Discover other titles by Jordan Silver

SEAL Team Series
Connor
Logan
Zak
Tyler

The Lyon Series
Lyon's Crew
Lyon's Angel
Lyon's Way
Lyon's Heart

Passion
Passion
Rebound

The Pregnancy Series
His One Sweet Thing
The Sweetest Revenge
Sweet Redemption

The Spitfire Series
Mouth
Lady Boss

Beautiful Assassin

The Protectors
The Guardian
The Hit Man

Anarchist
Season One

Eden High
Season One

What A Girl Wants
Taken
Bred

Sex And Marriage
My Best Friend's Daughter
Loving My Best Friend's Daughter

The Bad Boy Series
The Thug
Bastard
The Killer
The Villain
The Champ

The Mancini Way
Catch Me if You Can

The Bad Girls Series
The Temptress

Other Titles by Jordan Silver

His Wants (A Prequel)
Taking What He Wants
Stolen
The Brit
The Homecoming
The Soccer Mom's Bad Boy
The Daughter In Law
Southern Heat
His Secret Child
Betrayed
Night Visits
The Soldier's Lady
Billionaire's Fetish
Rough Riders
Stryker
Caleb's Blessing
The Claiming
Man of Steel
Fervor
My Little Book of Erotic Tales
Tryst
His Xmas Surprise
Tease
Brett's Little Headaches
Strangers in The Night
My Little Farm Girl
The Bad Boys of Capitol Hill
Bad Boy
The Billionaire and The Pop Star

Gabriel's Promise
Kicking and Screaming
His Holiday Gift
Diary of a Pissed Off Wife
The Crush
The Gambler
Sassy Curves
Dangerously In Love
The Billionaire
The Third Wife
Talon's Heart
Naughty Neighbors
Forbidden
Deception
Texas Hellion
Illicit
Queen of My Heart
The Wives
Biker's Baby Girl

Jordan Silver Writing as Jasmine Starr

The Purrfect Pet Series
Pet
Training His Pet
His Submissive Pet
Breeding His Pet

http://jordansilver.net

Kindle Edition, License Notes

Table of Contents

Dedication

This book is dedicated to all the butterflies that have followed me from the beginning, and those we have met along the way. Thank you for your continued support for not only me, but for all the Indie authors out there who you give a chance just at a mere mention. Thank you sincerely for being you. May we enjoy many more smutastic days together....

Chapter 1
Lyon
***

"It's the holidays, you know what that means, it means Kat and Elena are going to be starting their shit any minute now and I don't have time to fuck around. I can't keep them contained if they take a ride on the crazy train again this year."

"Colt, dude you have got to get a grip bro, every year it's the same shit with you. You let these women run you ragged." He shook his head and went back to work. We were in my home garage working on a bike for one of my kids and I was getting twitchy.

"Shut the fuck up, like they don't have you hauling shit you fuck." This morning Kat tried to trap me with the pussy as usual, which meant she wanted something, and since pussy was on the breakfast menu with kids in the house and a baby in the nursery, it had to be big.

I'm not sure as yet why she was sending out her lure, but my powers of deduction says it has something to do with the holidays. Every fucking year it's the same shit, my house looks like the North Pole upchucked and the grandparents lose their fucking minds along with their decorum.

Fifteen years and these fucks are still at it. Daniel, Drake and Cyrus try to outdo each other in the gift department and Elena turns my house into a bakery with her shit. I made the mistake of having one party at my house and now it's an every year thing.

"Well, what is it this time? We haven't even had turkey day yet."
"Don't you understand you ass? That's when it starts. You remember last year? Before the damn turkey had been digested they were planning a shopping trip and somehow I got dragged into that shit."

"Not for nothing Colt, but I think I prefer their shit to yours. It's nice to have a little peace and quiet around here without some crazy fuck gunning for us."
"And whose fault is that? Who was the one that foisted her off on me? I still owe your ass for that one." He still thought that shit was funny, the way he'd got one over on me

when he first introduced me to my wife, the woman of my heart.

"I'm thinking you came out on top on that deal bro, you owe me."
"What're you two talking about?" Kat appeared in the doorway at the top of the stairs. If I was in a good mood I would appreciate her beauty after all these years but I knew the little sneak was up to something and I needed all my wits about me.

"Nothing, go back inside it's cold out here." Nosy ass. She gave me a look like she'd heard every word before sauntering down the steps. She doesn't listen for shit. "Kat it's cold, you just had a baby back inside." She pouted but had the good sense to haul her ass back up the stairs.

"I just came to tell you that your parents are here."
"The fuck they want?"
"COLTON."
"What?" The older those two get the worse they become. Daniel was hitting the pipe like he thought it would stave off old age and Elena has taken her nosy shit to a higher level.

Between them, my wife and kids, I am so fucked. Kat and her fucking golden pussy got me into this shit.

"Jared, why is your boy looking at me squinty eyed, what am I supposed to have done this time?"

He laughed and pretended an interest in what he was doing. The fuck still thinks it's hilarious the way she runs circles around me. But this year I plan to put a stop to her shit. My life is paradise: I have a beautiful wife, six- count them-six amazing kids, and a business that's been growing every year.

The only fly in my ointment, are these very same things. My wife is a sneak, her kids, especially her daughters, are doing everything in their power to put me in an early grave and my business has exposed me to some of the dumbest fucks in creation. Now this one and her mother in law are trying to make my ass nuts.

"Katarina, whatever you and your mother in law have planned please leave me the fuck out of it. Tell that old lady I'm not doing shit this year but sitting on my couch and watching the game."

"You can tell her yourself and while you're at it you can explain to your kids why their holiday has been spoiled because daddy is a Grinch. Oh look, here's Catalina now." She had the nerve to grin before going back in the house; she'd set me up.

The leader of Hitler's youth came into the garage just then. To see this kid you won't be blamed for thinking that she's all that is sweet and wholesome. She looks like everybody's idea of the perfect little angel, down to the blonde curls that riot around her head, and her mother's unusually beautiful eyes. But in that chest beats the heart of an old despot.

"Hi daddy, whatcha doing?"
"Nothing kid what can I do for you?" She gave me her signature look, which meant she was about to zing me.
"Oh nothing, grandma's here and grandpa; guess what?"

Shit, that's her favorite drive daddy to drink game. "I don't want to guess why don't you just tell me?"
"Grandma said that we're all taking a cruise for Xmas."

"The fuck?"
"Ooh daddy you said the bad word." Her eyes had that light in them that makes me twitchy.

"Sorry baby come here, daddy didn't mean to say the bad word." I glared over her head at a grinning Jared, the ass. What the fuck is Elena doing? How the fuck was she expecting the weed head to last on a ship for that long without his stash? All I have to do is get dad on my side and put a monkey wrench in this shit. But first, when it rains it pours in this bitch so I knew there had to be more.

"What else did grandma say?"
"I can't tell you it's a secret." The little thief held out her hand palm up. I'd like to know where the fuck she learned the shakedown. I know you're not supposed to compare your kids, but this one is nothing like her sister, and she's worse than the boys.

"Catalina you wanna eat dinner tonight?"
"Of course what kind of question is that daddy?" she gave me her mother's eye roll 'daddy's stupid' look.

"Well, if you wanna eat and sleep here you'd better tell me what grandma said, now take your hand down." You have to be firm with this one, trust me; she's not like any five-year old you've ever met in your fucking life.

"Daddy, I don't think you can do that, daddies and mommies are supposed to feed their kids, it's the law, teacher said so."

Teacher has a big fucking mouth. "Okay then, if you don't tell me then I'm not getting you that chemistry set you want." "So? Santa will get it." "She's got you there bro, better give it up."

"Why don't you go on back inside Catalina you're giving me a headache." "Okay daddy but I'm pretty sure you're gonna wanna know what else grandma said." She hopped up the steps and turned to smirk at me. Where the fuck did Kat get this kid from?

"Told you some shit was up, now I just gotta wait for the other shoe to drop." I know my wife and this little act she's putting on ain't fooling me worth a damn. We went back to work on the bike for Aiden who was turning into his old man. The twins were like night and day. Quint was most likely going to be like his grandfather, the little fuck was into all things cop.

So while his brother wanted a new or faster bike every other week, he was more into playing investigative games on line or whatever his mother and aunts and uncles came up with to keep him happy.

"Daddy, uncle Jared, dinner's ready." My baby came down the steps an hour later. "Hey Caitie Bear, why are you all dressed up?" my daughter is turning into a beauty, not that she could help it with her mother being who she is, but I sure wish she would take it easy on her old man with this growing up shit.

"Todd's coming to dinner, grandma said I should invite him." And just like that my day got worse.
"His father lose all his money in the stock market?"

"Dude!" Jared shook his head at me. I glared his ass into silence. It seems that when it comes to my kid and this dating shit, everybody has an opinion that differs from mine.

My daughter was looking at me like she thought I was losing it. I'm pretty sure that's the impression their sneaky ass mother gives them whenever I veto one of her fucked up schemes, like I give a shit.

"Well, why is he coming to dinner?"
"Daddy, be nice, please. Don't you like my dress?"

"No, I like the way you dressed a few months ago, jeans and tee shirts." Her face looked like I'd slapped her and I felt the way I do when I know I've done something that hurt her mom.

"Don't look like that princess, come here." I hugged her and patted her shoulder. Why the fuck did nobody tell me that having daughters and a wife would turn me into a pansy ass? Half the time, I have to watch what the fuck I say. For a man who's accustomed to just letting it all hang out, that shit is fucking annoying.

I'm not about to lie though, I hate the fucking dress; it makes her look too grown up. I should burn the shits as soon as her mother buys them, or better yet...

"I think the dress looks really pretty Caitlin." Fucking sellout. His wife has his nuts at home in a lockbox, the fuck. In fact, out of all my guys, I seem to be the only one who kept theirs, though it's a constant struggle.

Kat thinks I don't know what the fuck she's up to. Since there's no legal castration these days, women have found another way to take a man's balls. They're sneaky about it, so you have to be on the alert at all fucking times, or before you know it, you'll wake up one morning and be a fucking eunuch. Walking around behind her at the mall with her purse in your hand and drool on your fucking chin. Fuck if I'll end up like that.

"Tell your mom that we'll be right there as soon as we wash up." She was not happy with me, I could tell, but she turned and went back up the steps. "I'ma bury that fucking Todd kid in the backyard."

"Colt, you worry me. She has to grow up bro, she can't be your little Caitie Bear forever; and I thought you were getting to like Todd? The kid seems solid to me, in fact to everyone else but you."

"That's because he's not sniffing around everyone else's kid but mine."
"She could do worse bro, some of these high school kids are fucking nightmares."

"That's the problem, if he was a dick I could fuck his shit up and be rid of him like that. But this one is like a fucking mother's dream or some shit. And no matter what I throw at him he doesn't fail, what the fuck am I supposed to do with that?"

"You're supposed to leave them alone you idiot, it's part of growing up. Don't you remember being that age?" I was out the garage and up the steps with him laughing and calling me back. "Kat, here, now." I bellowed every fucking word even though I knew it would get her thong in a twist.

"Colton, what is wrong with you? We have guests in the house."
"I give a fuck. They don't like my screaming they can head the fuck out. Listen, about these dresses and shit that you keep buying Caitie, cut it out." She had the confused look she gets when she's trying to pretend that my words have gone over her head.

"I don't get it."
"Okay plain and simple, the next time you walk into the store to shop for Caitie Bear pick up jeans, no maybe overalls, that might be better."

"Colt did you fall and hit your head, what's the matter with you? Come on in here everyone's heading to the table." Jared walked by us shaking his head on his way to the bathroom to wash up.

"Just do as I say or nobody's gonna be wearing shit around here." I know what the fuck I just said, but they're making me crazy. I went upstairs to my bathroom and got cleaned up before swinging by the nursery to check on our newest addition.

He is the result of one of Kat's little schemes. It would serve her ass right if I'd nailed her again this morning with her sneaky shit. Little Cody was asleep so I just ran my hand gently over his head and left the room. Time to go face Elena and her shit.

I was on my way when I ran into the little upstart that was fast becoming the bane of my existence, and my lovely wife, heading into the dining room looking all cozy. "Good evening sir, thanks for inviting me to dinner."
"Kid I didn't…"

"COLTON, that's okay Todd we're happy to have you." He went off somewhere, probably to go sniff around my kid. "The fuck are you glaring at, I didn't invite him, aren't you always harping about being honest with the kids?"

"That's not what I meant and you know it Colton Lyon. Now it's almost time for the holidays and I want you to behave. You're the one who started the holiday tradition remember, the year Caitie was born? You went all out, we can't change things now."

"Kat, I wanted to give my kid a nice holiday, I want to give them all that. But you and Elena have lost your fucking minds every year since, and this year I mean to put a stop to it." I left her fuming, or more like thinking up new ways to fuck with me, and went in search of the culprit.

She was fixing the table and lying to her grandsons about some shit or the other. That's another thing I noticed about my parents as grandparents, they lie their asses off about every fucking thing and seem to think that the things they wouldn't let their own kids do is perfectly okay for my kids to.

"Mom, I wanna talk to you."
"Oh, hi son, nice of you to join us dinner's ready, can you go find your father?"
"Where'd you lose him this time?"
"I don't know, you know how he is."
"Yeah, probably smoking up my damn basement with his shit." I caught myself halfway down the steps, her little errand boy. "What the fuck?"

Chapter 2
Lyon
***

I found the pothead in the basement in a haze of smoke. All I could do was shake my head, because there was really no point in saying, or doing anything. "Your wife's looking for you."

"Oh hey Colt, I was just taking a little breather, you know how your mother gets around this time of year." He rolled his eyes and put out the little end of nothing he had in his hand.

"Yeah, what I'm trying to figure out is why she's doing that shit here instead of at your house."
"Son, get real. You kids are all grown and gone, there's no one there in that big old house but your mother and I. She needs more than that for her holiday fix; besides, do you think I'm stupid? I know she'd run my ass into the ground with her shit, all it takes is a little bug in her ear to get her on the right track and there you have it."

"What the fuck? Are you saying you're the one who thought this shit up?"
"Boy, weed is not for running around and shit, I do enough of that at the hospital. A man smokes the good stuff so he can relax and feel good. Your mom has way too much time and energy and it doesn't seem like she plans on slowing down anytime soon more's the pity."

"So, I hit the blunt, tackle her for a little R and R and when she's nice and pliable, I drop some suggestions in her ear. She runs with it, gets your wife and sisters involved, so the rest of you yahoos have to deal with their shit."
"Sneaky fuck; I'ma hide your stash." He grinned because he knew I'd never be able to find all of his hiding places. "Barring that I'll put you in a fucked up home when the time comes."

"You poor sap, your wife and mine already discussed that and we're moving in as soon as the time comes."
"Moving in where?"
"Here of course, or wherever it is you and Kat end up. Speaking of which, you better be nice to that Todd kid, in a few years this is going to be you, you might end up on his doorstep. Our Caitie seems very fond of

him." The fucker had the nerve to grin at me.

"Got into a bad batch did you?" I left before he made me any more crazy with his shit; his wife could come and get him herself. I have to put an end to this shit whatever the fuck it was they were up to. Enough is enough I can't let a weed head outsmart me. And what was that crack about them moving in, had Kat lost her damn mind?

"KATARINA LYON." I don't think I ever yelled this fucking much in my life until she came along. She and her damn kids have robbed me of every ounce of peace and quiet I ever had, now she wants to sic her in laws on my ass, no fucking way.

"You bellowed your grouchiness?" She sauntered her little ass into the hallway where I was waiting for her out of earshot of the others.
"Cute, did you tell Elena and the pothead they can move in here when the time comes?" her look of guilt was a dead giveaway.
"Kat."

"Colton be serious, you're the oldest son, it's your duty to take care of them, and

I'm my parents' only child so we have them as well, and then there's Cy-Cy…"

"What the fuck?" The little sneak ran her hand soothingly up and down my chest and cooed at me.
"Come on Colt, we have quite a few years before we get to that, let's just enjoy today hmm. We have a lot of planning to do for the upcoming trip and…"

"Kat, I promise you, if you get me on a ship, half of you won't make it back."
"Oh stop it, it won't be that bad."
"We're not going on a cruise for the holidays and that's final."

"Well then, what do you suggest?" She was leading me back towards the dining room when Daniel came up the stairs with his clothes stinking of weed. I don't know how the fuck I'm supposed to keep my kids off the pipe when grandpa is a known druggie. How the fuck does that work?

Everyone but us were already seated, even Drake and Tina were here as well as Cy who was eyeing Todd pretty much the same way I do.
I took my seat but I was not a happy camper. In the last few years Kat have been running

circles around my ass and I've been letting her, that shit ends now, not my kid.

I don't know how they do it, but I'm pretty sure her mother and mine have been teaching her every dirty trick in the book. I just have to look at Drake and Daniel to see the end result, though Daniel seems to be just as slick, maybe there was something to staying high all the damn time.

The kids were excited at least, and dinner wasn't the nightmare I'd expected, until coming onto the end. That's when Kat and Elena started their shit. Now every year I get flustered and that's how they win, this year I plan to keep a clear head and stick to my guns.

I listened to them as they threw around ideas. The little one kept smirking at me and that's how I knew they were up to some fuck and that got me to thinking. "So what do you think Colt, does that sound good, a little change up from the norm?" Uh-huh, her smile was a mile wide let's see how long that shit lasts.
 "Kat we're not going on a cruise because I'm not buying the tickets." That was simple enough.

"Kat doesn't need you to buy her anything son, she has her own company remember?" Fucking Elena.

"Yep, but if I burn that shit to the ground then what?"

"Colton, don't talk like that in front of the kids, they'll think you're serious."

What the fuck, did she think I wasn't? "Listen you, I don't care what tricks you two have up your sleeves, it's not gonna work this year. It comes to mind that Elena is a Xmas freak, so I don't see her getting on a ship and going anywhere for the holidays. That means the lot of you are after something else; so you throw me a red herring to catch me out there with what it is that you really want."

"Since you want to be a damn sneak, we're doing Xmas my way. It's too late for me to keep you from fu…I mean mucking up Thanksgiving, because that's just around the corner, but this year everything will be done the way I want it for Xmas and who don't like that shit can stay the fu-hell in their own house." I glared at the pothead who wasn't looking too cocky now.

"You kids might wanna run along now before you hear something you shouldn't." I dismissed the kids before Kat accused me of scarring them for life. Her face looked like a storm cloud, served her ass right. I waited until the kids had cleared the room before turning back to the sneaky ass adults in the family.

"Katarina you know Hitler's little henchman still believes in Santa and now there's little Cody who still has years of that shit. If you don't want me telling your kids that fat fuck don't exist, you better not mess with me on this shit."

So what they were all looking at me like I was crazy, that's the way you have to do it in this house. The women stormed off to the kitchen with the dirty dishes, muttering under their breath. Good, at least I'll have some peace and quiet until they came up with some fuck else to mess with me about.

"Boy they're gonna make you pay for that one."
"Dad, I'm not you, I'm not afraid of Kat or Elena, and Drake. I would thank you to keep your wife out of my shit."

"I'm not getting involved, every year it's the same thing with you. You know they're gonna get their way anyway, why not just let them have it and be done with it? This shit gives me heartburn. I saw all the secret shit and late night phone calls, but I find me a corner and stay the hell out of the way."

"You need to hit one with me Drake, I'm telling you it fixes whatever ails you. Colton it would do you good to get in on this, you need to mellow out son, you're cracking up, haven't I taught you anything? You don't threaten these women son, it only makes them stronger, and more devious."

"Whatever, I know come D day Kat's ass better be in this house and my kids aren't going anywhere. The rest of you can go run around if you'd like." I wonder what the fuck they were really up to? I'm gonna have to bribe the little one for info, fuck.

***

Chapter 3
Lyon
***

I think they got to her first because she was nowhere to be found, but I wasn't about to go anywhere near Kat and her mother in law right now to see if she was with them. I helped the boys tinker around with their bikes some, and kept an eye on my Caitie Bear and the mini douche, before Jared headed for home, leaving me in Lyon hell.

Pretty soon, it was time for the others to clear out and I still didn't know what the fuck Kat, her mom and Elena had spent the last two hours in a huddle about. I said goodnight to my older kids and grabbed the baby who was acting like he had the eleven to seven shift somewhere.

The sneak came into the room not long after but was giving me a wide berth. Her ass was still upset, tough, that's what the fuck she gets for plotting against her husband with the enemy. I decided to fuck with her just because I could.

"Come here Kat." I shifted the baby to one arm and held the other out to her as I reclined on the bed. My son was a fucking drool machine, my whole damn side was soaked, and I'd only just laid him on my chest.

He was also half the size of his poor mother, who had lost her fucking mind and decided she wanted to try natural childbirth. I almost killed fucking Char and Elena for talking her into that shit, never a-fucking-gain. My heart can't take that fuckery no way no-how.

She took her sweet time getting to me but I let it slide. "Look at me; are you unhappy about something?" She shook her head no but her face was still not right. Now I'm a reasonable fucking man. I don't ask for much, just that my wife and kids are happy and content with their lot in life, and I do everything in my power to make it so.

"Is there anything you ever wanted or needed that you didn't get from me?" She gave me her puzzled, lost in the desert look but I wasn't buying her shit, she'd learned from a pro. Too bad for her little ass, I grew up with Elena's shit; I know all her plays.

"No Colton."

"Are the kids happy, they need anything?"
"Of course not, they're fine, we're all fine."
She reached over and brushed little Cody's hair.
"Then why the fuck are you moping?"
"I'm not moping."

"Yes you are, now cut it out. You know damn good and well you don't want to go on no fucking cruise. First of all, Elena would have a stroke if she couldn't decorate that damn tree of hers with her million and one grandkids around her, and there's no way you'd take our son on a cruise at this age so what gives?"

Uh-huh, she can't hide that guilty look for shit. "Spill it Kat."
"There's nothing to tell." Oh, so it was going to be like that was it? I kissed my baby boy on the head and laid him in the middle of the bed so I could deal with his mother.

"Katarina, you're always doing something that causes me to either beat your ass, or fuck you into submission. Now tell me what the fuck you and Elena are up to."
She started twitching and moving from leg to leg. I know what that means; she's not talking, so she's expecting a beating or a pounding, very well.

I got up and took the baby from the bed while her eyes followed me like a hawk on its prey. I gave my boy some shit to keep him occupied in his crib before heading back through the connecting doors into our room.

She backed up when I started pulling off my belt. "Strip." She looked at me, looked at the door, and down at her feet. "It's too far, you won't make it. Now this little infraction of yours I can't see how it deserves a beating. You didn't put yourself in danger so that's dead."

"But I want information and I know just how to get it out your little ass." I advanced she retreated. "I said strip." "Colt." She held her hands out in front of her and tried to ward me off.

"Kat, clothes, off, now." I flicked the belt in the air when it was finally free and her hands flew to her top. She kicked off her shoes and got rid of the rest of her clothes while I pulled my shirt off over my head.

"On the bed, hands and knees." "Oh shit." That's right, she knows what's coming. I'm about to make her pussy sing and learn all her top secrets at the same time. It's a win-win; then maybe I could get some fucking joy around here for the damn holidays.

I took a moment to enjoy the sight of her fine ass as it stuck up in the air, her pink pussy winked at me from between her spread thighs. I walked over and ran my fingers through her heat while my cock throbbed. He don't know the difference between teaching a lesson and just having a good time. All he knows is that the pussy, his pussy, is open and ready and he's ready to break out the gate at a run.

I got up on the bed behind her and spread her open. She was already half wet when I ran my tongue over her slit. That taste hit me right in the gut and I wanted to feast, but I knew she was hiding something from me and I needed to know what that was so the feasting was gonna have to wait, right now I was on a mission.

I licked her pussy until the juice coated my tongue and her ass began to twitch. I hummed into her pussy because the shit was so good, but I caught myself, I had a job to do so I pulled my tongue out of her.

"You'd better hold onto those sheets real tight babe." She had started to relax there a little when she felt my tongue. I think

I even heard her sigh, like she thought she had me.

I know she knows tongue fucking her pussy is one of my favorite delights, but I was after something else that was sure to have her giving up everything she thought she wanted to keep hidden from her man.

Leaning over her back, I bit her ear, just a small nip, just enough to send those little shocks to her nerve endings. "Tell me." "Uh-uh." She was playing stubborn, but it was no more than I expected. Taking my cock in hand, I ran just the pierced head up and down her cunt slit. She clenched and tried to pull away, but my teeth in her neck held her in place.

I sucked on her neck until I left a mark, all the while teasing her clit and slit with my cock ring. I let my fingers squeeze her nipple while her pussy juiced all over my meat and her ass went in search of cock, which I held back from her, barely teasing the entrance to her gash until I was ready.

"Oh shit Colt, please." I hadn't even started on her ass yet. This'll teach Elena to fuck with my shit, now I was going to fuck with her program. "You gonna tell me?" I slammed into her hard and held still. Her pussy twitched and squeezed around my cock while her greedy ass pushed back for more.

"Tell me." She shook her head and tried to syphon the juice from my dick but I had news for her ass. The more she pushed, the harder I pulled back, until just the tip was inside her. She started begging, pleading, but I turned a deaf ear. I needed her well and truly gone to get what I wanted, I was almost there.

Reaching around, I played with the piercing in her clit, while letting the tips of my fingers just brush her flesh, light as a breeze. She mewled and her pussy gushed. Any minute now! My cockhead leaked pre-cum into her pussy and ran down the backs of her thighs with her own juices, the mingled scents permeating the air.

I gave her short jabbing fucks with my heavy hard cock while tapping her clit and her breathing became erratic. I waited until she was close and changed shit up on her ass, keeping her confused and needy.

She grumbled when I pulled all the way out and screamed when I went into her ass. I had to push her head down into the mattress so that her nosy ass kids didn't hear her racket.

I fucked her ass hard for five minutes straight with no let up. I almost wished she would hold out on me so I could continue my assault on her ass, but she wasn't that strong. I didn't even have to ask her again, the constant teasing in and out of her ass, fingers on her clit, and stopping when I knew she was close did the trick.

"It's nothing Colton really, just um..." She stopped talking; just what the fuck was it that she was hiding from me? "Stop fucking around Kat, talk." I pulled her head back and sucked her tongue into my mouth while slamming her ass and fucking her pussy with three fingers. She was well and truly stuffed on all ends.

Her pussy was creaming hard so I knew she was close to a massive orgasm. I stopped all movement, except for the in and out of my fingers in her pussy. I flexed my dick in her ass and bit her again, hard enough to mark her in the same place as before.

"Caitlin wants to spend Xmas with Todd." The words ran together but I got it. "Say what now?" She really stopped me in my tracks with that one. Of all the things I expected to come out of her mouth, that wasn't even on the list. Now I was the one who had to keep my head on straight and think this thing through. Dealing with these fucking women is like walking a minefield.

"So you thought if you told me about a trip I would be more than happy to stay home and allow my baby to go to some fuck's house for the holidays?" Why did nothing these women did make any damn sense? Who the fuck thinks like that? Conniving fucks. I started moving inside her again, but slowly this time. There was more to this little tale I was sure.

"You might as well tell me the rest."
"Promise you won't get mad."
"I'm not promising shit, unless you want me to stop I suggest you start talking?" I gave her a few courtesy strokes to remind her of what she would be missing if I pulled out.
"I kinda told her it was okay."

"You what?" She looked over her shoulder at me. I guess the 'you're so fucked' tone in my voice tipped her off that she was in a fuck load of trouble. I could imagine what she saw on my face just then because pissed didn't even come close to describing what I felt.

"Colt…" I held her eyes for pure spite as I fucked into her ass until she was close, then pulled out and sprayed her back with my seed that she so did not deserve right now, before letting her drop to the bed.

She was pissed, but she had to know that shit was coming. "I suggest you tell her there's been a change of plans, or better yet I'll tell her." I fixed my clothes while standing at the side of the bed watching her fight her temper. She hated not having my seed inside her.

"Colton you can't, she's really looking forward to going." I gave her a look that usually shuts her ass up, before heading for the door. Kat's problem is that she lets her damn kids get away with shit. Now she'd just cost her daughter her little friend, because if that fuck thought he had enough props to invite my kid to have Xmas dinner with his family, he must know some fuck that I don't. Fucking teenagers and bullshit.

She jumped off the bed and came after me, but lucky for her, the baby had had enough of his own company and started fretting. "Go tend to my son before you get your ass beat." She knew not to challenge the finger pointed at her face.

Now, I have to go crush my kid because Kat's too fucking soft. Why would my Caitie Bear want to spend the holidays anywhere else but with her old dad anyway? Seems like I'm losing the pulse of what the fuck is going on around here. It's time I took the reins back before Kat and her fucking brood drove me insane.

"You do know I'm going to ban that little fuck from coming here right? That's what the fuck you get for being sneaky. Let me find out you and fucking Elena been teaching my kid to be a sneak like you two. I'll ban her ass too."

"COLTON."

Chapter 4
Lyon
***

I'd forgotten that it was way past bedtime and my kid was asleep. She looked so innocent, like my little girl. Why couldn't anyone else see it? When I look at her, especially at times like this when she's not looking back at me with one of her mother's patented looks, all I see is the little angel I brought home from the hospital.

She'd been that little girl for so long, even as she grew and times changed, she'd still been my Caitie Bear. But all that had changed almost a year ago when she met that boy. Now I'm lucky if I see the shadow of that kid.

It seems I spent as much time watching her sleep now, as I did her first two years of life. It's about the only time I have with her these days. That's not exactly true but fuck it's beginning to feel like it. She is so much of my heart, the first from my body. Mine and Kat's first creation, and she will always hold that special place in my heart.

I thought for sure that I would have more time with her before I had to deal with this bullshit though, but I guess it was a sign of the times. She was growing up too fast I wasn't ready to let go dammit. She's my baby girl.

I ran my fingers softly through her hair light enough that I didn't wake her. She looked so innocent, so perfect. Shit, if she was doing this to me, I wonder what the fuck Hitler's youth had in store for my ass. Now there was a thought to make a man's nuts crawl up his ass.

Since I was already up I decided to make the rounds and looked in on all my kids. I had to save my third son from certain death by putting him back in the bed that he was hanging half off of. The twins who were all but joined at the hip still shared a room. I pulled the covers up over them in their separate beds and walked out heading for Catalina's room.

My little terror had her thumb in her mouth as she slept on her side. I covered my grin with my hand as I stood over her. What a fucking con, she looked like the most harmless little thing. My baby, as much hell as she gives me I wouldn't trade her for the world.

I could stand here and look down at her like this, and just see it. This one is going to take my life in a whole other direction. I'm not sure why, and the baby was yet to be old enough to see if he was going to turn out the same, but of all my kids, this fucking kid got all of me in her. It was going to be fun to see what the female genes did with that shit.

I know one thing was for sure; she's going to give Kat a run for her fucking money. Serve her sneaky ass right, I should really let Marnie loose on her ass. She has no idea just how much like me Catalina really is, but Elena does, that's why she's always trying to hide from my kid when she's up to her shit.

She sighed in her sleep and rolled over, and I wondered what the fuck she was plotting in her dreams. As I left her room I said a silent prayer as I looked back over my shoulder at her sleeping form. Please let me keep them safe. It was the same prayer I said every morning when I woke and the last thing at night.

Things had been beyond anything I could've imagined these last few years. There was no danger lurking around the corner, no one was fucking with me and mine, and Kat and I were doing a pretty good job at raising decent well-rounded kids that any parent could be proud of.

The only thing fucking with me these days is Todd the teenage fuck, we have a love hate relationship. The fucked up thing about it is that I really do like the kid, in fact if he wasn't sniffing around my little girl, he's just the kind of kid I'd want my boys to be around. Fucking kid had a good head on his shoulders, was polite and smart as fuck.

Kat and Elena loved the fuck outta him, and he looked at my little girl like she hung the moon. That's what the fuck scared me. The kid is so fucking solid, how do I stop him and my daughter from crossing the line way before it was the right time for that shit?

Caitie Bear follows him around like he's her fucking lifeline. Kat says I'm jealous and though I'm man enough to admit that I don't like my daughter's affections being splurged on some little punk, there was more to it than that. She was too fucking young, a few months away from sixteen. Fuck, sixteen, I remember those years.

The other one was sitting up in bed with a pout on her face when I made it back to the master bedroom, following me with her eyes and shit like she wanted to fight. She's so fucking cute that even when she's working my nerves like a sore tooth I can't get away from that burning feeling of love that she brings to my heart.

"What did you do?"
"Nothing yet, she's asleep. Now you listen to me, I've been trying not to lose my shit around here with you and your damn kids, but this is the fucking limit. I don't give a fuck what your mother let you do when you were fifteen, but my fucking kid is not going to anybody's house for the fucking holidays. I don't even let your ass go anywhere what the fuck! And don't roll your eyes at me."

"I'm not…"
"Yeah, you are; you had to know that shit wasn't going to fly, but like everything else, you thought your ass could hoodwink me with the pussy. Now see where that shit got you?"

I pulled off my clothes, walked through to the other room to kiss my son goodnight and went to take a quick shower before going back to her. She was still sitting there working up a head of steam, stubborn fuck.

I climbed in bed and dragged her stubborn ass into my arms. She tried playing the stiff role, but a couple fingers in her pussy soon took care of that.
"You want a holiday ass whipping you keep your shit up Kat." I stroked her pussy a couple times before holding my fingers still inside her.

She tried to keep her movements, those little grinds into my hand quiet, but she wasn't fooling me. I grinned down at her after turning her onto her back. Biting into her jaw I pushed her legs open with my hips and settled in before sliding my cock home.

"Did I ever tell you how fucking tight your pussy is when you're mad? Nothing like it." Lifting her ass in my hands I fucked into her deep, making sure to catch her clit with the ridge of my cock.

She was pissed, but fuck, so was I. I was in the right mood for her ass. Stretching her arms above her head lifted her tits just the way I needed them for my mouth. She grunted when I sucked down hard, drawing her milk into my mouth. Her pussy liked that shit so I turned my attention to her other nipple.

I teased the shit out of her with my teeth and tongue while I used my cock to pile drive into her. It wasn't long before the pussy started juicing and those cute little moans she was trying her hardest to keep hidden were teasing my ears. "Whose pussy is this?" I knew that shit would fuck with her. She hates me right now so admitting that the pussy was mine wasn't gonna make her happy.

When she didn't answer right away, I pulled a switcheroo on her. Twisting my body at an angle, I fucked into her from the side, going past the opening of her cervix. She opened her mouth and I had to cover it before she screamed down the damn house. Then I pulled out and flipped her over, driving back into her until I found the spot I'd just left, right into the mouth of her womb.

Leaning over into her ear I whispered one word. "Whose?" all I needed to do was flex my cock so that the heaviness would hit her.

"Yours, please."

"Oh yeah." Getting to my knees, I forked her legs and with my hands on her hip, fucked her hard.

Her pussy took a battering and she kept her face buried in the sheets to muffle the noise as I fucked her without mercy. This time, when I felt that tingling in my balls, I buried my cock deep and flooded her pussy with my seed. Greedy fuck.

I rolled away and pulled her in as we both tried to come down from the heights. I'm gonna have to up my damn vitamins in to deal with her and her shit in the near future.

I'm pretty sure I'm going to have to do a lot of this in the next few weeks, because shit was about to get fucked around here. I had no doubt that she and her fucking posse will rally come sunup and be ready for my ass. I hope she knew that her ass was the one that was going to pay the price for that shit, because this time they'd crossed the fucking line.

As fate would have it, I wiped out the next day because my mind has been so preoccupied that I wasn't paying attention. Jared the fuck carried on like an old woman and sicced Kat and Elena on my ass when I refused to go to the hospital for a few scrapes and bruises.

Of course they pulled the guilt trip on me and I ended up in the damn doctor's office to be patched up, and no one was listening when I told them I couldn't take any time off because I had shit to do. The fuck stupid doctor went right over my head and told those two that I needed to stay put for a few days, and they crawled up my ass.

Chapter 5
Lyon
***

" Colton, you need to go talk to Caitlin." She was trying to sidetrack me. I've been laid up for a couple days with a bum knee and her little pussy hasn't caught a break once. "What do I need to talk to her about? What's wrong with her now?"

Fucking teenagers and hormones and shit; there's always some fuckery going on around here. She was busy folding sheets and looking ripe in short shorts and a tight tank. My dick was looking for round three. I had no interest in talking to anyone right now.

"Her little friend is moving away." "Which one?" Kid's got a ton of 'em she could stand to lose a few. I can't step foot in my place without somebody else's brat running in and out my damn house. "Todd."

I got the biggest fucking grin on my face. "COLTON! It's not funny."

"What, you want me to be sad that he won't be around to get his grubby little hands on my little princess?" After the whole holiday dinner debacle, I'd had a strict talking to with my little girl. She'd given me the cold shoulder for a day or so but that shit hadn't lasted long and sap that I am I had relented on the ban I'd had in mind. Now this shit was like my early Xmas gift.

"Why the fuck is she sad anyway? Don't they have I this and I that so they can keep in touch? Is he moving to Outer Mongolia or some fuck?" I wish. I'd come to tolerate the kid because he really looks out for my little girl, but I was never gonna be okay with anything with testosterone anywhere near my daughter.

"Sometimes I worry about you. Now go in there and say something to her." What the fuck was I supposed to say? Hey kid better luck next time? The fuck! "I'll get to it in a minute, get over here, you said five minutes ten minutes ago, now you're sending me on errands and shit."

"Go first and I'll come." I gave her one of my looks that still packed a punch. "Kat my dick isn't about to wait another second more. Get over here or explain to your kids why it sounds like daddy's killing mommy. I will do you rough. One, two..."

"Okay, okay, keep your shorts on." Fuck that I took them off before she made it to the bed. Can't go around naked in my own room these days because the little one is always sneaking in and out of shit. "Lock the door before your nosy ass daughter come snooping in here and shit."
"You want me to get on top this time? Don't want you hurting that old knee or anything." She's got jokes I'm about to show her old. I pulled her down on the bed beside me laughing her damn head off. She still makes me so happy it's stupid. "Hey babygirl."

She sobered and smiled up at me. "Hey my Lyon." I growled and pounced on her. She's still the hottest fucking thing in creation. The years haven't changed that, having six kids didn't either. I look at her and I still see the same tight ass that she conned me with all those years ago at the BBQ. The sneak.

"Touch me Colton."
"Where?" She'd gone all soft and sweet on me and my heart ached.
"Here!" She took my hand and placed it on her tit. I felt the nipple pebble under my

hand as I pushed my leg between hers. So much heat. I lowered my head and took her nipple into my mouth, teasing her with soft nips until she pulled on my hair to get her way.

"I'm gonna eat your pussy but you can't make a racket, you know your damn kids are gonna come running to my damn door with their shit."
"I'll try but I'm not making any promises."
"Fine, I'll just put the pillow over your head."

I made my way down her body looking for the goods. Her newly shaved pussy, which I'd taken the pleasure of shaving myself the night before, winked at me. I took one long lick over her clit while easing a couple fingers inside. She was already juicing and squirming and I hadn't even really got started on her yet.

Lifting her fine ass, I brought her up to my mouth and dug deep with my tongue. My cock was sending out signals, he knew what was waiting for him and wasn't in the mood to wait. I maneuvered my body so that she could reach me with her mouth. She bit my cock ring before licking the pre-cum from the head and taking me into her throat. "Fuck." She was trying to one up me again.

All it took was a finger on her clit while I tongue fucked her and I was back in charge. I knew her body as well as my own and used that knowledge to bring her to the brink and held her there. "Colton that's mean."
"You wanna cum?"

She growled at me and pounced, rolling me onto my back being careful not to hurt my knee as she climbed on and forced my cock into her wet cunt. "That's right baby take it." She braced her hands on my shoulders and lowered her tit to my mouth.

"Move that ass baby." I helped her along with my hands on her ass, rocking her back and forth on my cock. She still loves a deep hard fuck but I had to make it quick. With a house full of kids I've been left hanging way more than I like, so to get us both off before the fucking brigade trooped to my door, I flipped her over, fucking up my knee in the process and pounded the fuck out of her pussy until we were both climbing.

"Fuck Kat, you fucked up my knee again." I rolled away from her huffing like a bull in the ring.

"I told you to let me get on top old man." I smacked her ass hard and she bit me, still a pain in the ass. "Now go talk to our daughter, she's very upset."

I ain't doing shit but taking a nap. A man can't ask for more than this, three rounds and still some more in me for later. A wife who still makes me feel like a king every time I touch her, shit I've got it made. I just have to keep her ass occupied between now and Xmas and we're good to go.

"Colton!" Damn she likes to yell. "Yes my little flower." She rolled her eyes at me because she knew I was giving her shit. "Go." Fuck! She don't forget shit.

So what the boy was moving away, it wasn't the end of the world. I hadn't heard anything about Caitlin going to his house for dinner since that first night, and he'd been scarce around here since I was laid up which suited me just fine. Maybe his damn parents had caught a clue and found shit for his teenage ass to do around their place instead of hanging around mine.

All the same, I climbed off the bed and went to clean myself up so I could go see my kid before my annoying ass wife nagged me to death with her shit.

Chapter 6
Lyon
***

"Hey princess how're you doing?"
Damn she looks so sad.
"I'm fine daddy."
"You sure, anything you need to talk
about?" She shrugged her shoulders and
picked at her nail. Shit, just like her mother,
talking to her is like pulling teeth.

"Okay then if you're sure you're
okay." I turned to make my escape but I
should've known better dealing with Kat
number two.
"Daddy." Shit she was tearing up.
I'm gonna kill that little fuck for making my
princess cry. "What is it baby? What's
wrong?"

I walked over and sat on the bed next
to her, wrapping my arm around her. She put
her head on my shoulder and her hand on
my chest. Still daddy's little girl. Why
couldn't she stay little and sweet for at least
the next thirty years? Why did she need to
go getting mixed up with boys and shit?

"He's leaving daddy, he's moving away and I'm just going to die if I don't see him again. You have to do something daddy please."
What the fuck? What the fuck has this kid been doing with my kid? If I find out he's been doing more than holding her hand on my couch, I'll bury his ass in the backyard; lil punk.

"Baby, you're not gonna die, come on. You'll make other friends, it's not as bad as all that. What about all those nice girls that are always here eating me out of house and home…"
"DADDY…"
"What?"
"It's not the same thing, he's my boyfriend, we're in love…"
"You're in what? KAT…"

She came running on the double. "What, what's happened?"
She looked at me like she thought I'd killed our daughter or some shit. If anyone was in danger of being strangled it was her little ass. "Your daughter just informed me that she's in love. How the fu…how did this happen?" She rolled her eyes and walked over to hug Caitie bear, taking her out of my arms. "Don't roll your eyes at me woman, I

wanna know what's been going on around here."

"Colton, calm down nothing's going on geez. Caitlin it's going to be okay, stop crying now, you'll only make yourself sick." I watched as my wife soothed my daughter's breaking heart and felt like an ass.

I didn't know what the fuck I was supposed to do about the kid leaving town, or more to the point what my wife and kid expected, but I didn't like her hurting like this. I left the room when they started whispering, I probably had five minutes to spare and I was gonna use that time to check on my shop. Anything to get away from dealing with my baby telling me she was in love.

The little one gave me a knowing look when I came out the bedroom. What the fuck was that about? "You scare me kid." I'm gonna have her mom have another talk with her. She's probably been listening at doors and shit again.

"Catalina, don't you have homework, a science project, some form of mass destruction to plot?" I spend more time in the principal's office with this one than at my shop. I had to tell the asshole principal if he suspended my kid for being a kid I'd cap his ass.

What the fuck they expect to happen when they put a nosy ass, inquisitive, troublemaker in a lab? It's all her mother can do to keep her from burning down the house with her shit. Now they got this higher learning bullshit for advanced kids, and this one conned them into thinking she's a brain and they let her loose in their school. Good for their ass.

They tried selling me on some home schooling bullshit, but they're fucked. From the hours of eight to three, Monday to Friday she's theirs. As long as she's in one piece when she gets off the bus in the evenings, I give a fuck.

"Daddy, what's wrong with Caitie?" Shit, here come twenty questions. "Nothing." "Then why is she crying? And why is mom…" "Catalina go read a book." "That's boring, so, is it Todd?" Her eyes widened to the size of saucers. Nosy fuck.

"What it is, is none of your business." She gave me her mother's patented look and walked away. But not before one last parting shot.

"Fine then, be mean; I won't tell you what's been going on."

Shit, she got me. Apart from causing chaos and mayhem, she's my little snitch. Watergate ain't got shit on her. "Come 'ere pumpkin." Damn, I wonder what this is gonna cost me. I wish the women in my life weren't so damn sneaky.

She gave me a sweet angelic smile as she made her way back to me, but there was no hiding that look in her eye. This kid is going to be on the evening news one day and she won't be the one behind the desk, damn. What the fuck happened to my life?

I followed her back to her room where I knew she was going to fleece me again. At least once a week she cons me out of something. She's good at what she does. She collects info all week and corners me when she's ready for a trade. Fucking spooks will probably be knocking at my door before she's thirteen. They'd either be looking to recruit her or haul her in for espionage or some fuck.

***

"Elena, what are you and your posse doing here?" It was two days later and I'd come home a little early to a full house of nosy ass women. My knee was the least of my worries and I'd told Kat as much when I went back to the shop. Between her and her damn kids, it's a wonder I hadn't ran away the last few days, always some fuck going on.

"We're here for Caitlin."
"Caitie Bear, what's wrong with my kid?" I walked to the fridge to grab a bottled water. From the looks of it this one planned to stick around and I wanted no part of it.
"We're having a little female intervention. You know she's not doing so well with her boyfriend moving away." I'ma kill this old lady swear to fuck.

"She doesn't have a boyfriend." I felt a headache coming on.
"Of course she does, you know Todd."
"She's fifteen, she doesn't have a boyfriend; what the hell is wrong with you people?"
"Oh Colton grow up, she'll be sixteen soon.
"You wanna get that little fucker killed keep talking shit in my house."

"Listen son, you'd better get your act together or you're gonna drive her away.

Next thing you know she'll be moving across the country to live with him and we'll lose our girl, all because you're too bull headed to get with the times."

Fucking girl hasn't even finished high school and already mom had her married off and living half way around the country. "Are you people trying to drive me crazy? What all are you lot supposed to be doing anyway?" I would tell her to get the hell out, but she won't do it and then I'd have to listen to her daughter in law the rest of the night with her shit about my behavior.

"We're gonna have a spa day, the whole works. Then we'll have pizza and ice cream because that's Caitlin's favorite." "Where's your dope head husband?" I couldn't listen to any more of her shit or I'd lose mine.
"Oh he's somewhere back there with the boys, you know how he gets when he's around them. Only one thing Colton, can you maybe take Catalina out somewhere for a couple hours?"

"Why?" Shit, she was trying to stick me with the spawn.

"Well you know she's rather inquisitive, and I just think Caitlin needs all our attention now, just this one time, please."

"Hah, no." Hell if I'm gonna take my little spy out of the works, how else am I supposed to know what the hell goes down at this little impromptu party of theirs? Just then the other one came into the kitchen.

"Oh hi honey I didn't hear you come in. Come on Elena the rest are waiting." She tried giving me a little peck like that shit was gonna work after being gone for eight hours. I bent her double and laid one on her, while my nosy ass mother snickered like a five year old. "Kat what's going on around here, what's this about an intervention?"

"Well it's not really an intervention per-se. We just want to make Caitie feel better that's all." This shit smacked of Elena and her meddling ass. I gave her the look that she's been ignoring all my damn life, fucking woman.

"I suggest you and the rest of your crew pack your shit up and head out. Caitlin isn't suffering from anything that a good grounding won't cure. I already spoke to her; this boy moving away is not the end of the world. She wants to act like her life is over, six weeks in her room should cure her of that shit."

I left the room before they could beat me over the head with their moral indignation outrage fuckery. I give a fuck. My kid's been moping around here like someone had died and shit for the past few days. Every time I looked at her she gave me the sad eyes.

There wasn't shit I could do about the lil punk moving, but she seemed to think there was. And since daddy always made everything right in her world, she was expecting the same this time too. Daddy was happy as fuck with this turn of events thank you very much, and wasn't about to do shit even if there was something he could do.

***

Things calmed down or seemed to for the next little while and I hadn't heard any more about the lil punk and his move. I wasn't sure what was going on there since he was still sniffing around my kid every damn evening like clockwork, but at least my little girl wasn't looking like death.

Xmas was nipping at my heels and I hadn't heard shit about any secret missions so I was breathing easy again these days. There were no phone calls from the school telling me to come get my kids, and for once it looked like my life was gonna get back on track for the holidays.

"Kat where's Catalina?" I don't even want to think about why she entered my mind just then. I'd heard the boys, seen Caitie Bear, but realized I hadn't caught a glimpse of my little shadow ninja since I came home. If she wasn't eavesdropping, or banging away at that piano, her pothead of a grandfather gave her to annoy my ass, then who knows what the fuck.

"Oh crap, I haven't seen her since she came in here while I was feeding Cody. She was trying to tell me something about one of the boys and she was fit to be tied, but the baby was fussing so I didn't really pay attention."
"Well fuck." I passed off the baby who was nodding his head half asleep and left the room almost at a run.

Chapter 7
Lyon
***

"Catalina, what're you doing?"

"Oh nothing." I found her puttering away in the corner of my workshop in the basement. The same space she'd conned me out of a few weeks ago when she was spilling state secrets. I'd been sidetracked by a phone call on my way to search her out half an hour ago and all but forgotten. "Why does your 'oh nothing' smell like sulfur?"

"It's nothing daddy, just a little experiment."

"Uh huh." I'm finding a convent for her ass first thing.

"Guess what daddy?" Oh fuck.

"What baby?" I wasn't getting anywhere near whatever the fuck that was she was doing. I was already biding my time to make my escape. Maybe her mom knew what the hell she was up to in my basement.

"Aiden pulled my hair and called me a brat."

"He what?" I was headed back up the stairs for his lil ass. He knows the rules; never put your hands on your sisters.

"Oh daddy don't get mad, get even. That's what nana said."
"Which one?" I stopped in my tracks, that shit don't sound too good.
"Nana Elena." She gave me what I can only term as the Dr. Evil grin.
Shit! Fuck, what was she making over there anyway?

I got out of dodge and went looking for her mom. I passed Aiden on the way and pulled him up short. "You hit your little sister?"
"Dad she glued all my baseball cards together, then she did something to the bike because I told her she couldn't have a ride."
Shit, that was bad, still. I gave him my best father stare. The little shit tried to stare me down but that shit wasn't about to work. The women in this house might run my ass but the boys get no play.

"Sorry dad, I'll go apologize." He hung his head and looked none too happy about it.
"Better wait on that one kid, I think she's making up some kinda witch's brew for you."

"What? Dad, last time she did that I lost my hair."

"Dem's the breaks son." He followed me down the hallway griping.

"Well what am I supposed to do?" I think everyone was scared of my Catalina, I can't say that I blame them.

"Call Daniel and Elena or Drake and Tina, maybe one of them will let you live with them 'til she calms down."

"Daaaadddd, do something."

"I'll think about it, now you'll remember next time not to put your hands on your sister."

"But she's always..." He caught that look again and piped the fuck down. "No excuse, ever."

"Yes sir." He slinked off to his room and I went to find the wife. She was in the kitchen already, cooking something that smelt almost as good as she did. I walked up and wrapped my arms around her, rubbing my ever-ready cock into her ass and she turned her lips up for a real kiss. She smelt like baby and heat and I loved her so much it was stupid.

"By the way, Catalina wants a puppy." She turned back to her pots.

"No."

"Come on Colton, I'm surprised none of the others have asked before now. Why can't our little girl have another pet?"

"Do you have any idea what that kid can do with a puppy?"

"What's she gonna do with it?"

Like she don't know. Our family dog was too big for her to fuck with thank fuck, but a puppy, hell no.

"Kat, I don't know how to tell you this but that one's just not right." I tapped the side of my head so she'd get my meaning. As usual when I said anything about her badass kids she got pissed. "I wish you'd stop saying that."

"Too bad, it's the truth. She's either gonna live with us for the rest of her life, or she'll be doing fifteen to life in the near future. Do you know what she's doing right now as we speak?"

"A school project, why?"

"School project my ass, she's concocting something to fuck with her brother for pulling her hair." I have to admit that's some shit that I would've done, but if this kid turns out to be that much like me, my ass was toast. The others were all pretty manageable but that one? Fuck me; it was like doing penance or some shit. "Well did you stop her?" Shit.

KAT
***

"Elena, it's not going to work I'm telling you, he's on the warpath." I waited until later that night to make the call.
"You leave him to me I know just how to work him."
That's what she thinks, that's what she always thinks, but it never happens quite the way she plans. And why after all these years do I still follow? Because I'm holding out hope for that one time we actually win.

Colton Lyon has not changed, in fact he's grown worse with time not better. Every year he finds some new way to torture me, and the kids and curtail our freedoms to the point that going to the supermarket is a national security experiment. Nothing gets by him, and I'm pretty sure he has half the town spying for him.

I feel bad for poor Caitlin because I know that when the time comes for her to leave the nest, which no matter how much Colt tries to put it off will be in the next few years, there's going to be hell to pay.

"I'd better get off the phone now before his highness catches me and goes off on one of his tirades again. Please do whatever it is that you've got planned soon, Thanksgiving is in a few days and before you know it it'll be Xmas and the kids need an answer soon."

I don't see what the big deal is about Caitie spending part of the day at Todd's. The boy has dinner with us at least once a week, but Caitie has never been allowed to go to his house in return. Colt seems to think that I'm such a dunce that I don't know about teenagers and that somehow I'm going to let my daughter run wild.

Little does he know that we've already had the sex talk and I'm satisfied that my daughter has a good head on her shoulders. He doesn't know we've had the talk because he'd have a conniption if he ever found out that I mentioned the word sex to his precious firstborn before she was at least twenty-one. I've never seen....

"What the fuck are you plotting now?" See what I mean?

"Nothing whatever gave you that idea?" I hurried and hung up the phone.

"Who's that, Elena?"

"Yes."

"Uh-huh, whatever the fuck it is it won't work. I have to make a run today you need anything while I'm gone?"

"Just a husband with some understanding, that would be good for a change."

"I've got understanding Kat, I understand that if you don't stop your shit your ass isn't gonna be able to sit for a week. The last time your nosy ass kids looked at you cross eyed for days, I don't think they're gonna buy your excuses this time."

"Colton, can you please go do whatever it is that you're doing, you're making me tired."

"I'm not making you shit, it's all that sneaking around shit you and mom are always doing. No wonder dad hits the pipe as much as he does, it's his escape. Well you're not turning me into a fucking pothead, it's going to be your ass every time."

I had to change the subject quick before he got it into his head to get things out of me. He's been on high alert since the last family dinner, and like I'd told Elena we had to move soon if we were gonna get Caitie her last Xmas dinner with her friend before he moved away. I wouldn't push so hard if it weren't important to her, but it was. I knew just the thing to take his mind off of stuff.

"Daddy, I need stuff." Saved by the child.
"Dammit..." He cut himself off as he looked around at our youngest daughter. "Didn't I tell you about sneaking up on me? How long you been slinking around back there?"

Watching the two of them was like taking in a comedy act. I think little Catalina is the only breathing thing that actually makes Colt sweat, and she does it so effortlessly too.

"I wasn't slinking daddy honest, so you gonna get me my stuff?"
"What is it?"
"Just stuff for school."
He looked at the piece of paper she held out to him like it was going to bite him, before taking it from her and unfolding it. "What the hell are you going to do with sulfuric acid?"

Oh boy. She stared up at him, all him, that's what their problem was. This one child of ours for whatever reason, was the carbon copy of her dad. I can't wait for the day he figures that out it ought to be good.

"Daddy it's for my science project." "Your teacher gave you this list? Kat get that school on the phone, what the fuck are we paying them for, to turn this one into a criminal?"
"Colton I'm sure there's been a mix-up I'll handle it, don't you have to go?"
"Trying to get rid of me are you, I wonder why."
"Nobody's trying to get rid of you-you paranoid person."

He was getting red in the face again and mumbled something as our girl walked out the room. I don't know what I'm gonna do with this man, he's gonna give himself a coronary and what I was about to tell him was only gonna set him off again; might as well get it over with.

***

Chapter 8
Lyon
***

I needed to go. My boy Law had just called and said I needed to get to his place and from the sounds of it the shit was serious. "Catalina's little friend is coming over to work on a school project together isn't that cute?"
It was the 'isn't that cute' that tipped me off. "What little friend?" Her cocky grin told me I was not going to like what came next and I was right.

"You know, one of her many boyfriends, she told me this one might be serious so she invited him over to work on their science project together."
I glared at her for half a second before stalking her across the room. "Didn't I say no girls; huh? Didn't I know this shit was going to happen?"

"Who in the fuck is this kid and what science project?"
"Some volcano thing they have to work on, calm down. Your father promised to come

over and help you know he's a science buff."

"Yeah that's all we need is to get somebody else's kid high."

"Oh pooh you know he doesn't do that around the kids stop it."

"I know they'll be high as a fucking kite messing around with him. And I'm not sure about Mengele and her little pal in my basement building shit. Kat why are you trying to make me crazy?"

"Colton honey you need to calm down." I growled at her ass and left the room.

I left the house after my crew got there and headed to Law's place. He'd sounded like some fuck was up but I can't imagine what that could be. And when we rode up a few hours later my antenna zinged off the charts. The place looked like they were gearing up for some shit and it didn't look good.

"The fuck Jared, is Law planning a coup? Look at all these military type fucks, shiiiit." I slid off my ride and went to meet my old friend who'd had some trouble of his own not too long ago, with some asshole offing his parents and kid sister.

We'd offered our services of course but he wanted to handle shit on his own. Now his yard looked like they were planning a raid on Fallujah or some fuck. We shared our usual greeting before getting down to shit. "What's going on brother?" I asked him if this was about his family, something I was more than willing to help him take care of, but once again he denied it. It was the way he skirted the issue whatever it was, that started the burning in my gut. That's my warning signal, my first inclination that some fuck is way off.

When he told me to stay Cool, he had to know that the opposite was gonna be the result, there was some fuck going on here that obviously involved me, but what the fuck could that be? Law and I hadn't ever really made any runs together. I've made bikes for him and some of his guys before and we developed a kind of bond over the years. Though he was way younger than I, he was my type of people.

Creed, I'd done a few save the children runs with in the past, but I didn't know the soldier types Law introduced me to. He didn't have to tell me they were military that shit came through their pores for fuck sake. When he came back from talking in hushed tones to one of them, probably the leader, he led me off to his clubhouse office, and my whole world got turned the fuck inside out.

My men lined the wall behind me because they got the memo that some fuck was up. "Okay Lyon, the rest of us have had time to look at this shit in the last day or so. I'm gonna show you what we've got and then we're gonna decide what to do next. As it stands we have more questions than answers…"

What the fuck? "Bro, you're starting to make me nervous, I don't like being nervous, just tell me what the fuck…" He passed me an album and I still didn't know what the fuck, until I came to my daughter. "Caitie bear? What the fuck is this? Who the fuck are these kids?"

I heard his words of explanation but my mind was already back at my house. I flew out of my chair and went to make some calls. When I came back into the room I was ready for all out war.

I thought I had problems with my kid wanting to spend Xmas with a boy, what I learned that day showed me how fucking insignificant that shit was. For a split second my world literally tipped on its axis and everything faded to black. When life came back into focus I saw red, the blood of the motherfuckers who'd done this shit.

Someone had put my daughter in a fucking flesh rag. All I could think about was getting back to them and making sure she was safe. I'd made some calls to safeguard my family while I was away and dealt with what I had to until I could get back home, but it wasn't the same as me being there.

The day dragged on forever while they brainstormed about what to do, me, my mind was already made up. Somebody was gonna die. When the name Porter came up things started to fall into place and I had my target.

The others had their own shit going on, some ring they were trying to break, and though I empathized with their plight I didn't give a fuck. My only interest was in taking out the fucks who'd put my daughter in this shit.

I didn't let on, not after my first outburst, but all the while I was there I was plotting. They wanted to wait, to go after some fuck that was in the hills hiding out with the hate brigade as Law calls them, fine, I'll play along…for now.

By the time they'd decided on something I was ready to grab my piece and head to the desert. I wasn't leaving here without some answers and from what I'd gleaned from their conversation this Stockton fuck that they'd mentioned was in the hills, looks like I was headed there after all.

There were too many unknowns involved since Law had called in his military friends and they had different ideas about how to deal with shit than I did, but as soon as I had time to think this shit through I was going out on my own. No way I could sleep at night with this fuckery out there.

Tyler, one of the ex SEALs, seemed to have his shit straight, so he's the one I picked because I knew he would go for my play. I had my boy Travis Mallory get me some info that these boys wouldn't be able to get their hands on no how, because his old man owned practically everyone in the known world, well the fuckers that mattered anyway.

While Logan, the leader of the SEALs was more level headed, which I respected no doubt, I just didn't see the need for that shit in a situation like this, Tyler and I had our own understanding. I wanted to move on this shit now, not stand around plotting strategy fuck that. Dead is dead I give a fuck how they get that way.

I couldn't let myself think about anything but the end result, because when my mind stopped I saw my baby girl's face in that fucking book, her and a hundred other innocents. The mention of the Porters as one of the players only made things more pressing for me. I'd ended their son for fucking with my wife years ago, now the family was after my kid.

No one knew for sure what had happened to Porter, but I'm guessing his family suspected, I give a fuck. His raping ass got just what he deserved and now it looked like the mother, father and uncle were heading for more of the same. His idiot girlfriend hadn't fared too well either, but I wasn't the one that ended her, my boy Travis had taken care of that one as a favor.

All fucking day while my family was at home unaware that their lives were being turned upside down I sat there and listened to every bit of information I could gather. Not because I was even remotely interested in doing things the way these boys had planned, but because I still needed to know all the players.

There was mention of some desert fuck who they believed was the mastermind, the puppeteer, he might be out of reach for now, but it seemed there were more than enough assholes stateside that needed dealing with.

That night my crew, Ty, Creed and Travis snuck off since we were of the same mind. The hate mongers were hiding out in the hills around Law's place and they were apparently hiding the guy who had had the album back in Georgia. The shit was confusing as fuck, but from what I gathered that's why the SEALs were involved, this guy Stockton was their mark and they'd followed him here.

Creed had a dog in the fight because some asshole had put his woman in the book as well, and so was Law's and one of the SEAL's. Everybody had a stake in this shit, but these boys were trained to do shit systematically. For me, there's something to be said for the berserkers, I have some of that shit running through me because I just want blood in my throat.

"Fuck Law." He and his posse came out of the bushes once we made it away from his compound. "Your wife ratted you out bro." Fucking Kat, I knew when I called her that last time she would be listening to my voice to gauge the situation. She's sneaky like that, if I'm not giving her what she wants, she reads me to get it anyway. He wasn't stopping me though no one was.

When he and the SEALs were through pontificating it was time to go. "Let's go." I followed Ty because we were after the same fuck, while Creed and Law had other targets. The rest of the SEALs went into the fucking trees like smoke, spooky fucks. My mind was razor sharp as we hunted down our prey. I was only after answers, because we'd already established that this asshole was nothing more than a pawn.

Ty worked him over first and then it was my turn but the sight of the fuck sent me into a deep dark place. When he told me that the Porters were behind my daughter being sold or auctioned or whatever the fuck was the reasoning behind that book, he was already a dead man.

I'd just thrown a fuck over a cliff and didn't think twice about it, I'd do it again and probably would have to before this shit was over and done. By the time we made it down off that hill I'd only just wet my appetite I wanted blood.

I wasn't planning to head back tonight, Law had captured some of the hate fucks and I'm guessing he was planning to work them over for answers, but my sneaky ass wife needed me home.

I had what I needed anyway, and though I was willing to help them do clean up when the time came, I wasn't about to wait around cooling my heels while they did their thing.

I told them as much before heading out, I needed to get home so I could have eyes on my little girl, reassure myself that she was safe. I had time on the ride to think about the last fifteen years. I hadn't even thought about Porter at all in all that time and had done everything in my power to erase him from my wife's memory.

How was I going to tell her that this shit was back to bite us in the ass? She didn't even know that I'd offed that fuck for what he'd done to her and I wasn't about to tell her, neither was I about to let his asshole family fuck with me and mine.

I had some hard thinking to do. Here I was thinking my family was safe and all the while someone had had my daughter marked for who knows the fuck what. I didn't like the feeling of desperation that threatened to overcome me. I've spent my life protecting my family from the darkness of the world. Whatever it takes I'm gonna make sure that my wife and kids are never touched by this shit.

Caitie Bear, my little girl, every time I thought of her I saw her little body as she toddled towards me, her eyes bright with glee as her daddy held out his arms to catch her. She was going to have everything she wanted in this life and no motherfucker was going to take that from her.

This family, these people that were involved in this shit were never gonna get close enough I'd kill every last fuck if I had to-to keep that from happening. Jared and the others that had come with me wanted to head to the desert now and take care of shit, they weren't too fond of waiting around either, but I needed to regroup. It was the holidays; Caitie's little life was already in turmoil because the boy was leaving and now this. What does a father do?

By the time I made my way back home later that night I'd forgotten all about Xmas and whatever the fuck it was Kat was up to. Life had just thrown me a hard curve. I'd pushed hard to get back to her because she was worried. She knew me well enough that when I called her she heard it in my voice no matter how I tried to hide it. The fact that I'd put men on the house and taken the kids out of school would be more than enough to get her antenna going haywire.

***

I came into the house in the dead of night and she was waiting for me. "It's okay baby, I'm home." I held her to me as she shook and fought back the tears she knew I hated. "How're my kids?" She nodded her head against my chest telling me that everything was fine. "Let's go look."

I held her hand in mine as we made the rounds. I didn't want to give anything away, but as we stood over our eldest my knees almost went weak. As long as I live I'll remember seeing her face looking back at me from that page; that was something I couldn't, wouldn't share with her mother.

I kissed her little head and silently vowed once again, to stand between her and whatever may come her way. I took my wife to bed and made love to her like it was the first time. "Colt, what's wrong, won't you tell me?"

I could only shake my head at her as the emotion threatened to choke me. "I love you so much Katarina, my Kat." I kissed the place where her heart beat, light butterfly kisses, before taking her sweet tit in my mouth and tasting her milk. It was like taking a part of her into me when I fed at her breast like this.

Her hands held my head in place as I made love to her with my mouth and tongue, moving back and forth from tit to tit until I had my fill. "You want my mouth baby?" I wanted to fuck, wanted that ultimate connection. But I knew when she was feeling like this she liked her man to take her away, all the way.

I made my way down between her thighs and inhaled her scent. Her pussy has its own scent; it's all her, my own personal aphrodisiac. I sucked her pussy until she was begging me to fuck her, and in that moment when I slipped into her, we both forgot everything else but each other and the way we felt when we were joined together like this.

"Look at me." I held her head in place as I rocked my cock into her. There were no words needed, as we loved each other. We just held on and let our bodies do the talking. By the time I was emptying my seed inside her I felt whole again.

Chapter 9
Lyon
***

The next morning she questioned me up one side and down the other about my run the day before but I didn't share. "Why don't you focus on Thanksgiving babe, isn't it like in two days or some fuck?" I planned to stay around the house today and the kids were staying home. They were going on break in a few days anyway so it shouldn't matter.

"No, I want you to tell me why we took the kids outta school and why Tommy and the others have been staked out in my kitchen all night."
"No."
"Colton, are we in trouble?" I hated that tremble in her voice, hated that she was worried.

"No baby, you know I would never let anything happen to you, but there's some shit going on that I thought it best to have my family where I can keep eyes on them for the time being. It's nothing for you to worry about, I want you to go ahead and enjoy your holiday and don't give this shit another thought."

I went around the place making sure we were secure and then I went to work getting everything I could on the Porters. I haven't given those fucks a thought in years I was too busy living the life I'd carved out for me and mine. I can't say I was surprised that they'd come back after all these years to fuck with my happiness, that's karma for ya. But the fuckers should've come after me instead of my kid. Now their destruction will be ten times worse.

"You're still worrying Kat you know how I feel about that shit, cut it out. If there was something for you to stress over I'd tell you, but this, this is nothing that I can't handle. Stop giving me that look." Sometimes she sees too damn much.

I almost wish she was still harping on my ass about Caitie and her asshole friend. I wished even more than she would get moving on her Xmas bullshit whatever it was, all the shit I'd just spent the last coupla weeks arguing with her about. Anything but the worry and fear I saw in her eyes.

"Why don't we spend the day doing something with the kids huh? We can make a fire in the cold ass back and toast marshmallows or some girly shit. Maybe I'll take the boys for a run on their ATVs, you think they'd like that? We'll wait and see what our little pre-convict wants to do because you can be sure it's neither of those things."

I was trying to lighten the mood, but like I said, after all these years together, never being apart, she knew me as well as I knew her. It was getting harder and harder to tell her not to worry and have her actually listen, but I was gonna try.

***

Kat
***

Ha, he's not fooling me, I know him too well. I watched him all that day and the next as he hovered around me, and the kids like he was expecting us to disappear any second. I would call Law again and grill him but two things stopped me. One, he's as tight lipped as Colton, and two, Colt would lose his mind if I went behind his back like that. I guess all I could do is wait and see.

The kids didn't think anything of staying home a few days early, and Colt was so good at shielding them they never suspected a thing. They ran around the house like hooligans all except Caitie. Since Todd was leaving in a little over a month, the only time she had with him really was at school and when he came over in the evenings to do homework together.

My poor little girl looked haggard and miserable and it broke my heart that I couldn't do anything for her because her father is a maniac. I tried not to worry and by midday of day two, when nothing happened, I let myself breathe again. Colton on the other hand was in and out pacing like a caged animal. He and dad were closed off in the study for hours and I still didn't know what was going on.

I had to put it away, Colt was right, Thanksgiving was coming and I had a lot of prepping to do for the annual dinner that had somehow gravitated to our home instead of his parents. The house was usually like a revolving door on that day since we had everyone over including the crew.

"Colt I have to run to the store." You would've thought I'd screamed fire the way

he reacted. "Write me a list." I knew that
was coming but couldn't resist pulling his
chain. "No that's okay, you always forget
something I think I should go, I should've
already taken care of this by now but things
have been so crazy lately…"

"Fine we'll go to the store give me a
minute." He left the room and I heard him
barking orders on the phone before he went
outside to where he had men surrounding
the house. Next thing I know there was what
sounded like ten bikes pulling into the
driveway. "This is the limit, Colton what is
going on?"

"I told you, I'm just taking
precautions because of some stuff that's
been going on in the area there's nothing for
you to worry about." Yeah, I believe that.
We looked like a motorcade on the way to
the damn supermarket but my husband, who
drove like we were on the run was still
trying to convince me that all was right in
our world.

I know how he operates, I also know
that as long as there's breath in his body
nothing and no one would ever get next to
the kids or I, he'd proven that time and
again, but that didn't stop me from wanting
to know just what we were facing.

Because the holidays were right on our doorstep and there was always so much to do, I was being pulled in two directions. The kids always looked forward to this time of the year, they were already making noises about Santa and what they wanted most this year. How do I keep them from realizing that something was going on with all the changes?

Colt wouldn't worry about that his only concern would be our safety, so I guess it was up to me to keep things from getting too crazy. "Baby." He took my hand as we turned into the parking lot that looked like everyone had had the same idea at once; the place was full.

"Do me a favor huh, why don't you let me worry about our protection and safety and you take care of the festivities. I promise you that if there were something for you to worry about I would tell you. We straight?"

"I guess Colton I'll do my best, but promise me that you're not gonna be hurt either."
"You can take that to the bank."

***

Lyon
***

The next day, as I've been doing since coming back from Law's, I was preoccupied at the shop. People were hounding me for their shit because the holidays were coming, but my heart wasn't in it. Thank fuck I had a crew who knew what they were doing.

I sat at my desk with my mind in turmoil. This time of year is very important to my family they go all out. I do all I can to see that they have whatever they need, but this year I'm not so sure. With this shit hanging over my head, I don't know which way to turn. That's a lie, I want to go shed some blood to keep my family safe, but there's more going on here than just the threat against mine. Usually, I wouldn't give a fuck, but I keep seeing those little girls looking back at me from those pages.

There was one thing I could do while I cooled my heels, so I picked up the phone. "Mallory, you got anything new for me?" I knew if he did he would've called me already but it was something to do. I hate this shit; and now Kat's on my ass about Caitie Bear and that little punk.

This morning she'd started in on me again but a good stiff back shot had taken care of her ass, and by the time I pulled out our son was making enough racket to wake the dead, he needed the tit. That was enough to get her mind back on track.

"Not yet, the old man is still digging. I can tell you that this shit stretches farther than we thought. I don't know what this family is into, but the way it's looking, we're gonna have to watch our sixes if we get mixed up with these fucks. Me, I'm all in, that's my Goddaughter they fucked with so as soon as I hear anything it's a go."

"Okay man thanks. How're Lydia and the kids?"
"Fucking pains in the ass as usual." The smile in his voice was unmistakable fucker is as gone as I am. "You guys hear anything from my woman yet about their yearly madness?"
"Yeah, Lydia's been busy wrapping gifts. How many fucking kids you got bro?"
"Well seeing as how I started before you and you're almost caught up I don't think you have fuck all to say to me about that."
We talked shit for another five minutes before hanging up and I went to help the

guys. It was going to be another long fucking day.

Because I couldn't be away too long even with my guys on the clock watching the house, I cut out early. All the kids were tagged and I could see their every movement as well as my wife's from the watch on my wrist, but it wasn't the same.

When I tagged my family with the little chips in their jewelry, it was for the off chance of 'if' something happened. This shit with Caitie Bear in a fucking flesh rag was a definite threat, and the players were such that I wasn't taking any chances.

"Oh for fuck sake." Elena and her posse were here as was evident by the line of luxury cars in my damn driveway. I'd forgotten what day it was, tomorrow was Thanksgiving, which meant I was going to be overrun by these women all damn day with their cooking and baking shit.

Just as I expected, my kitchen was a madhouse. I looked at my wife in her element; she's the only reason I put up with this shit every year, because it makes her happy. "Ladies, hi baby." She grinned at me because she knew how uncomfortable I was around Elena's hen pack.

"Well Colton, it sure has been a while since we've seen you where've you been keeping yourself?" Ms. Lucille, one of mom's oldest and dearest stared at my ass like it was her next meal while asking me that innocent question.

"I've been around, Kat you good, you need anything?" She shook her head while fighting laughter and I stole a quick kiss before breaking out to the sound of laughter and wild suggestions. I could hear the kids running around laughing and having a good time, which helped to smooth the rough edges, except one.

"Hi baby what you doing out here all alone?" Was she ever going to lose that sadness from her eyes? Did she have any idea what I would do for her? There wasn't anything that I wouldn't give to make sure that her happiness was complete.

"I'm okay daddy. Daddy can I ask you a question?"
"Sure baby, you know you can ask me anything." Please don't let her ask me about that boy? Why are the women in this family trying to send my ass to jail? Don't they know me well enough by now? How can they not know that I would bury this fuck

somewhere if he looks cross eyed at my daughter?

"Why don't you like Todd?" Ah fuck! "Because I'm never gonna like any boy you bring home." What I'm supposed to lie to my kid now, what the fuck? She looked like she wanted to cry but I hardened my heart against that shit. No way was I giving the okay for my little princess to go off with some boy to have dinner. That smacked of commitment and all the other bullshit that she was not allowed to do until she was thirty fucking years old. Shit, my gut hurt.

"But that's not fair what did he do? Mom says he's just like you and nana Elena said he acts the way you used to when you were little." What the fuck? "Well that might be all well and true, but you're my little girl and I'm not ready for all this stuff. When I told you it was okay to see him, I…" Damn. "Look baby I'm sorry that your friend is going away but I can't lie, I don't want you being that serious about anyone at your age. I do like the boy, he's a nice kid, but like I said, he could be the king of Siam and I still wouldn't want him for you, do you understand?"

"I guess, mom explained it to me, you're being a dad and dads freak out about their little girls. But could you maybe think about it? I'm gonna marry him one day you know." She gave me a cute little smile while she ripped my heart out.

"Aw kid what're you trying to do to me?" She sat in my lap and rested her head on my shoulder the way she used to when she was a little mite. "I love you little girl never forget that. There will be times when I do things that will make you mad, like this dinner deal, but it's only because I love you and I will always protect you. You believe me?"

"I do daddy, but that doesn't mean I have to like it." So much like her mother. "Fair enough." She went off looking a lot better than when I first walked in. I tried to make my escape when I heard footsteps behind me. I'd know that walk anywhere.

"Oh Colton, may I have a word?" "Char, I'm not in the mood for any of your hoodoo crap." She grinned at me and I got a good look at her eyes. "Aw shit, you and your partner in crime got into dad's stash again?" Fucking women are always high and up to some shit.

"I don't know what you're talking about." She sniffed like I'd affronted her or some shit.

"I wanted to talk to you about this little situation…"

I felt the hair on my arms stand up, this one creeps me the fuck out. "What situation would that be?"

"You know; that thing that you and your boys are looking into. It's going to all work out. By the way, you have some very handsome friends, are they coming for the holidays?"

What the fuck? "Char, your husband know you cruising in my kitchen?" I beat feet outta there before she could work any more of that shit on my ass. Fucking tealeaves.

There was only one place to hide from this horde, so after I checked in with my guys who assured me that all was clear on the home front before I sent them off, I headed downstairs. There was no use in arguing with my wife and her mother in law because they don't listen for shit, but as soon as my house is clear I'm gonna lay down the law.

Chapter 10
Lyon
***

Thanksgiving went off without a hitch and now we were in the homestretch for Xmas. Kat was still not acting right but I put it down to this holiday crap. I had my eyes and ears open while doing my best to shield her and the kids from everything that was going on. The kids were back in school for the next few weeks and that was giving me some problems, but I found a way around it.

The days are getting better since I've lost that feeling of impending doom. For a minute there, I was seeing danger around every corner, drove Kat and the kids batty with my over protective shit but they'll get over it. "Kat where your kids?" Fucking house was too quiet, that could only mean the little fucks were up to some shit they weren't supposed to.

"They're in the house Colt, where you expect them to be? Ever since you put us all on twenty-four hour lock down they hardly even go in the backyard."

I wonder what her problem is? I watched her walk around putting away the baby's clothes and muttering to herself. That's what she does when she's gearing up to ask me some shit she knows I'm gonna knock back.

I walked over and wrapped my arms around her from behind. "What's on your mind little girl?" She felt so good, after all these years holding her in my arms still makes my heart do crazy shit. Fucking women, they grab hold of you by the balls and dig in. You would think that shit would taper off at some point, but everyday I still wake up and give thanks that she's mine. I still look at her and remember the first day I saw her, the real her, and it still gets me every time.

"Nothing's on my mind Colt." Lying ass. "I love you baby." My babygirl still melts when her man gives her the words, funnily enough when I try to show her by buying her shit she acts the hell up, that doesn't stop me though. She's got more diamonds than the Smithsonian.

She turned in my arms with her soft eyes. I brushed the hair back off her face and kissed her brow, we were having a moment. One of the few we can steal these days with her horde always in my shit. "I love you too Colton, thanks."

"For what babe?"
"For making my life so happy."
"Dammit Kat, I told you about that crying shit." She didn't do her usual grin and sniff into my shirt and I got worried, especially when she cried even harder. "Baby what the fuck? Tell me what's hurting you." She squeezed me around the waist and held on, sending my pressure up a few notches.

"Nothing's hurting me you crazy person." This time she wiped her nose in my shirt and kept her head buried in my chest. "I know something's bothering you, and if when you get around to telling me I don't like it, it's gonna be your ass."

"Why did you go to Law's place? And why after you came back you had the place surrounded like we were under attack?"
"You on that again?" I unwrapped the sneak's arms from around me and moved away. I know that's not it, because I know that my woman knows I've got her covered and nothing will ever get through me to get to her. She's trying to sidetrack me so it was best to beat feet before she pesters my ass

into telling her shit that she didn't need to know.

I'd played around with the idea of telling her, but between Law's place and home had changed my mind. In all our years together I've never burdened her with anything and I wasn't about to start. That cherish and love shit goes a long way, I don't think worrying her half to death about our eldest would be keeping up my end of the bargain. Plus when I off these fucks she'd probably put two and two together, and it was a given that they were not too long for this world.

It's funny, but for years people thought I was something that I wasn't. It took having her and our kids to bring that side out in me. I don't wanna go around offing fucks, but if they're out to do me and mine all bets are off. I give a fuck. I was halfway out the door before she called me back.

"Come back here Colton Lyon."
"The baby sleep?"
"Yeah why?" I tackled her and she screeched.
"Shh." I covered her mouth with my hand as I bore her down to the bed and followed. " I like these little skirts you been wearing

around the house, sexy." I growled into her neck as I lifted her skirt over her ass.

"This is gonna be quick." I pushed aside the skimpy ass underwear she wears to make me crazy, fished my dick outta my jeans and slid home. "Don't move babe." I reached around for her clit with one hand and her tit with the other, manipulating her flesh until I felt that liquid heat coat my cock from tip to base.

Then and only then, when I knew her body was ready to take me did I start fucking. "I'm coming in deep baby don't scream." I lifted her leg up onto the headboard, opening her up for my cock and fucked in on an angle hitting her spot. "Ahhhh, Colton…"

"Bite the pillow baby damn." I looked over my shoulder to make sure the door was closed and locked. Once I was sure that we weren't going to be invaded, I went to work on her. I held her head down in the bed as it creaked and banged into the wall.

No matter how many times I enter her, no matter what my day held, there is no feeling like being inside what's mine. "What're you up to?" I whispered in her ear as I held my cock still, letting it thump away inside her. "No fair quit it Colton." She squeezed my cock and rotated her ass back and forth on my dick and I forgot what the fuck I was saying.

"Bad girl, move that ass like that again." She laughed her special laugh that she saves just for our bed and I felt my heart ease a little more. Whatever it was that was bothering her it couldn't be that bad. I let loose on her pussy and she tore the sheets off the bed.

When she threw her head back and her mouth opened in a silent scream, I pressed down on her clit and let go. "Oh yeah baby right there." That felt like one of those breeding fucks but I won't be the one to tell her that shit since I'd already caught her ass with Cody. She tends to get snippy when I slip one by her.

***

Kat's up to some fuck again, I don't know what it is yet but I'ma fuck it outta her. One hard stroke and she'd tell me anything, but I'm biding my time. Char and her shit got me thinking. Every year we have a big shindig at the house. Usually my crew and Mallory and his kids would drop in, but I never thought to invite Law and his people.

Maybe this year I would, we could all do with some merriment after the last few weeks of bullshit.

I found her and ma in my kitchen whispering about who knows what when I got home one evening and braced myself. Not for nothing, but there's hardly ever a time when these two are huddled up that my ass doesn't end up in the middle of some shit I want no part of.

"What're you two up to now?" The way they jumped apart told me all that I needed to know. "Okay what is it let me have it." I folded my arms and leaned against the wall staring down the both of them. They shared a look and twiddled their thumbs. "Speak now or forever hold your peace ladies, Kat."

"Uh, well, we were trying to come up with a way to give Caitie a nice Xmas. As you know Todd's leaving the day after and she's been very despondent lately." How did I know this was about that damn kid? I wondered why my little girl had stopped moping around and bugging me about him, now I figured it was because these two had told her they were gonna work me.

"She's not going."

"Yes we know, you've told us about a hundred times already, but since you've had the kids on house arrest for the last few weeks and they haven't really had time to say goodbye, we figured you'd be a little lenient. But, knowing how hardheaded you are, we thought maybe we could invite him and his family here instead."

Elena gave me her best mother's look like that shit was gonna sway me. Since I knew the two of them wouldn't stop until they got something outta me, and truth be known, I wasn't as worried about the little shit as I was before seeing my baby in that damn book, I was feeling a bit magnanimous.

"Tell me something, what is it with you two and this kid?" I left my post on the wall and pulled up a chair next to them. Kat got all nervous and shit and Elena studied me like I was in the interrogation room. There was a lot of throat clearing before either one of them decided to talk.

"Well Colton, since Caitie knows that you go into an epileptic fit when it comes to her and boys, she tells me things."
"Things, what kinda things?" My growl had them both sitting back hard.

"You see, there you go, I'm trying to explain something to you and already you're ready to jump. Just listen okay, and don't get all bent out of shape before you hear the whole story."

"Okay, keep talking." Like I don't have shit else to do around here. "Okay, so do you remember that first time when Todd stood up to the bullies? Well there've been other things since then. Colton..." My face must've looked like a thundercloud. "What other things and why am I only now hearing about them?"

"Well Colton, son, the fact that you're gripping that chair arm hard enough to break it should give you an idea." Elena gave me a stern look like I was five and she was two seconds from sending me to time out. I give a fuck. I've had about all I'm gonna take when it comes to my kid. They couldn't know that I'd decided that the next motherfucker to even look at my little girl cross-eyed was gonna get fucked.

"Tell me Katarina." She wasn't looking too sure now but the bull was out the pen and there was no putting him back in. "Okay um, you know a couple months ago Todd went away for the school trip, they were gone for two weeks?" Yeah I remember-I remember having to run my kid off the phone at all hours of the damn night because of the time difference where he was or some shit.

So what the little fuck was smart and got to go off somewhere or the other to show off his brain skills, he still wasn't good enough for my kid.
"Well while he was gone something happened." I could feel the red haze covering my eyes. Not because something had happened, but because my wife hadn't told me about it.

My stare got her to pick up the story again. "These boys sorta kinda cornered her, not really it wasn't like that COLT…" I was out my damn chair like a shot, my heart was beating the fuck outta my chest. I hit the stairs running and headed for Caitie's room.

She was sitting on her bed with headphones on listening to music while leafing through a book. Why is this shit happening to me? Why can't these fucks leave my family alone? I started to go in and ask her to tell me what had happened, but she looked so young, so happy, I didn't wanna spoil that.

She's so damn beautiful, is that why? It had taken days before I stopped seeing that flesh rag every time I looked at my little girl. Now everything that involved her was magnified in my mind. I can't forget what happened to her mother when she was just a little older than she was now herself, and though I don't hold anything against Drake, I'll be fucked if anything like that is gonna happen to my kid. Not on my fucking watch.

By the time I turned around Kat was upstairs. "Where's ma?"
"She had to go what did you say to Caitlin?" She tried looking around me into the room but I backed her up until we reached our room. "Nothing yet, I'm waiting for you to tell me the rest."

She started that hand wringing shit and bit into her lip. Usually the lip biting thing would make my dick hard as fuck in no time, and I wasn't sure she wasn't doing it to distract me. "Stop that." I pulled her lip out from between her teeth.

"The boys thought it would be funny to tease her you know, they um, took her book bag and wouldn't give it back, things like that, and one of them asked her out and when she said no he said some ugly things to her."

"I'm gonna fucking level that school, who was it?"
"Colton I took care of it, the kid said he was sorry that he hadn't meant to scare her. He was embarrassed Colt that she turned him down in front of his friends."

Is she out her fucking mind? "I don't give two wet fucks Kat."
"Colton shh; Caitlin doesn't want you to do anything, don't embarrass her." She grabbed my shirttail to hold me back from leaving the room.
"What the fuck are you on Kat? They fuck with my kid and you expect me to do what?"
"But Colt they're just kids…"
"Who waited until the boy left to start their shit with her again, fuck that."

"Colt…"
"Kat, grab the baby and stay up here."
"Why, what're you gonna do?"
"Nothing for you to worry about peacemaker. Catalina come here." I yelled out for her not knowing where the little spook was.

"Yes daddy?" She came bounding into the room three seconds later, which meant she'd been listening at doors again and shit. I walked out of the room with her on my heels.

"I need you to make me up a batch of some shit." Her eyes grew big and there was a light in them that I hadn't seen since I'd seen it in my own when I was a wayward youth. Well fuck; while I'm saving a college fund for the others I'll be starting a bail fund for this one; I can just see it now. Plus she has some of Kat in her; this whole neighborhood is fucked.

"What do you want it to do daddy?"
"What do you mean pumpkin?" she took my hand and started leading me down the hallway.
"We…l…l do you want a hair remover, a rash, or something more permanet?" She couldn't even say the word but she sure as fuck knew what it meant.

"Permanent like how?" I stopped and looked down at her.
"Tell me first daddy." What the fuck did I get myself into now?
"Uh, I don't want it permanent."
"Then you don't need to know."
"What the… KAT."

"What is it now?" she came out the room and glared at me.

"You been watching after this kid?"

"Of course I have what kinda question is that?"

"How does she know about making potions and shit that can do permanent damage?"

"I don't know, she gets that from you."

Everything's my fucking fault around here; except when they're dong the right thing, then they're mommy's little darlings.

"Daddy you want me to help or not? I was busy."

"Busy doing what, listening in at keyholes? Didn't I tell you about that shit?"

"Daddy, I don't do that, you were yelling. Now you want me to do it or not?"

"Do what; Colt what are you two up to?"

"None ya."

"Catalina?"

"Nothing mommy, I'm just showing daddy my new trick." Damn she was good; if I didn't know what we were just talking about I would believe her. She had the innocent little angel act down.

"Kat, you sure they gave us the right one at the hospital?" I had to say that shit out the side of my mouth because she hears everything with her nosy ass.

"Colton."

"Just checking. Come on Mengele let's go show daddy your new trick." They have to be a boot camp or some shit that would take this kid.

I don't care what Kat and her mother in law says, I'm not letting these little punks get away with fucking with my kid. I followed Hitler's youth to her little science corner in my basement and listened as she told me about all the different products she had in neat little rows.

I'm thinking it's a good thing I did that because some of the most innocent shit you'd find in any household apparently could be used to destroy shit. "Catalina where did you learn all this stuff?"

"I read it in grandpa's book." She was busy mixing shit in a beaker with her little tongue caught between her teeth in concentration. "So what are you making there?" I was beginning to rethink this shit; maybe it wasn't such a good idea. What the fuck was I thinking getting my kid involved in this shit?

"Oh this, it will make you sick if you eat it in your food, not bad sick just make you go to the bathroom a lot-lot-lot." What the fuck! How the fuck do I get outta this? "Listen kid I changed my mind." She really scares me no joke. She gave me a put upon look and walked over to the sink to pour out her concoction. I watched to make sure it was all gone but what was the point? She'd whipped up her little batch like a pro.

I headed back upstairs to her mother. "Kat don't keep things from me again, anything happens to my kids I wanna know immediately. Did you talk to the principal?"

"Of course and the boys were reprimanded but I didn't want to make a big deal because these days they kick kids outta school for the littlest thing."
"Their asses need to be kicked out. I'm surprised that you of all people are taking this shit so lightly. They cornered her Kat."

" Colton I know what you're saying, but the way Caitie described it, it didn't sound like anything more than high school horsing around. The kids are gonna face those things babe, it's just a part of life." She can keep that shit. I don't trust these little teenage fucks.

I decided to snoop around and get the names of the kids who'd messed with my kid. I wasn't gonna do much more than put fear in them and warn them to stay the fuck away from her, but if my wife knew she'd raise hell. She still wears rose tinted glasses and thinks people are redeemable. I say they're all fucked in the head young and old.

Chapter 11
Lyon
***

When I wasn't dealing with Kat and her kids, or killing myself at the shop trying to meet quota, I was thinking up ways to fuck the Porters. It wasn't my style to let things wait this long and it was killing me, but things were finally moving thank fuck.

Old man Mallory had come through with some shit this afternoon that I felt I needed to share with the guys from the meet, but I had to wait until the coast was clear before I could start that conference call. The people in my house, especially the ones that were missing a chromosome are nosy as fuck, there's no telling who's listening at the door and shit.

"Hey Caitie Bear." I caught her at a rare moment when her damn shadow wasn't around, and barely stopped myself from asking where he was. That's some dangerous shit in itself. I've grown so accustomed to seeing those two together, that although I wouldn't dare mention it to my wife, it feels off when I don't see him sitting in the little alcove off my kitchen doing homework with her.

"Hi daddy." She smiled bright and closed her book, patting the seat next to her for me to sit. I'm a grown man, some might say a hard ass, but when my little girl smiles at me like that, and wants my company, I'm putty. "What you doing there baby?" I sat and put my arm around behind her.

When I look at her I see the best of me, and Kat. I see that first year of loving and fighting and getting to know each other. I see me panicking the day she came into this world, scared the fuck outta my mind. Never knew it was possible to love this damn much, doesn't seem like a body could hold that much emotion.

"I'm studying for the SATs." What the fuck? Isn't that what you do when you're leaving high school to go off to college? She still had two more years. "Come again." I didn't want to freak out because around here that's grounds for hilarity. Fucking Kat and her kids always find something to laugh at my ass about.

"Why are you doing that now? I thought that was next year or the year after."

"No daddy, remember? I told you and mom weeks ago that I had to take a test and if I did really well they would let me take them early. I passed daddy isn't that great?" What the fuck is going on in these schools? I went to school with motherfuckers that didn't graduate until they were staring nineteen in the ass. Granted they were dumb as a stump but what the fuck? Because my kid was smart I had to lose her a couple years early? We'll just see about this shit.

"That's real good baby daddy's proud of his smart girl." I kissed her hair and hugged her shoulder; still no awkwardness. I was waiting for the day, dreading it more like, when she wouldn't want her old man's hugs. She prattled on about some shit some girl at school had said and what some other one had done, and then of course I had to hear about Todd and some funny thing he'd done or said and my eyes started to cross.

I sat with her for a little while and did the dad thing. My sons were upstairs somewhere. I knew this because the little fucks were trying to jump through the flooring up there with their shit. I hadn't seen hide nor hair of Kat the sneak. "You finish your homework baby, I'm gonna go look for your mother."

"Okay daddy." Her head was back in her book and I stood in the doorway and watched her for a few seconds more, wishing like fuck that these moments weren't coming to an end anytime soon. Fucking kid owns my ass.

I found her mother, my wife walking around the living room with the baby in her arms trying to put him to sleep. My boy smelt me and picked his head up. "Oh good you're home, here." She passed the kid off, pecked me on the lips and tried to escape.

"Not so fast you. You tell my kid she could graduate early?" She rolled her eyes. "It's an option Colton."
"I opt no."
"Seriously Colton, you'd really keep her back? She's worked really hard for this, you can't..."
"She'll be sixteen, that's too young for her to be going off away from us." I wasn't even thinking about the assholes that were after her, them I can handle. But once a kid heads off to college that's it, they never come back. I was not ready for my little princess to fly the coop.

"You do know that that's what school is for right? And that it's a good thing that

'Our' kid is doing so well. I spoke to her teacher and she's way ahead. If we keep her back now it might do more damage than good."
Fucking woman always has an answer for everything.

"I gotta sign anything to make that shit happen?"
"Colt…" Uh-huh, I ain't signing shit. I rubbed my face against the baby's head and held him close. "How was he today, still colicky?" She's so good with the kids sometimes it seems I'm just ballast. I don't know how she does it either what with running her company from home and keeping the house in order. I help there of course, but somehow my little contributions never seem to be as much as hers. She does it all, my little wonder woman; pain in the ass.

"He's doing better aren't you baby? She made cooing noises at Cody and he giggled and rutted around in my arms. "Fuck Kat, what're you feeding this kid? He weighs a ton." The lil freak hefted her tits at me and grinned. I smirked at her because we both knew I got about just as much of that shit as he does. "I can vouch for that, I think I put on a coupla pounds myself."

We both had a good laugh at that one before we talked about our day. She'd stopped pestering me about my visit to Law's days ago and although she hadn't told me what it was that was bothering her she seemed fine and at night when I watched her sleep, she wasn't restless so I'm thinking we're good.

Things have been smooth sailing on the home front thank fuck, none of the drama that is usually running rampant around here with a houseful of hardheaded fucks who took after their mother. No one had broken any bones lately and the school wasn't calling us to complain about some shit that had nothing to do with me.

I don't know how many times I have to tell them whatever these kids do on their time is their headache. As long as they don't put hands on my kids, we're straight. But every other week at least there's a call for a parent teacher's meet. The fuck, I live there?

Chapter 12
Lyon
***

Later that night, when the house was quiet and I knew Kat's ass was down for the count because I'd fucked her into the springboard, I snuck into my office to make the call I'd been waiting all day to make.

"Hey Law, it's me, you're gonna need to call Creed and them military boys in on this one."
"Why what's going on? No Dana Sue go back to sleep. Hang on Colt let me get to where we can talk."

I heard ruffling and kissing noises and then he was back.
"Tell me."
"I got some Intel from old man Mallory today about our little situation."
"Hang on let me conference."

Shit went dead for a second and then I heard ringing on the other end. "Yo."
"Logan it's Law, I got Colt on the other line says we need a conference hang on I gotta call Creed." What the fuck! more dead air

and then another hello. Sounded like we interrupted Creed.

"This had better be good or some fuck's gonna get it."
"Creed we gotta talk Colt has something."
There was some mumbling in the background and another grown man had to explain to his owner why he was leaving her in bed. Fucking saps, the only ones that seemed up and ready were the military fucks and who knows what the fuck they'd been up to before we called.

"Okay everybody here, or you boys need some more time to placate your women? Fucking leashed."
"Shut the fuck up Lyon, I've seen you with your woman you don't fare much better."
Creed laughed and the rest of them joined in. We shot some shit with each other before getting down to business because I was pretty sure that they knew whatever was coming wouldn't be good.

"What did you hear?" That was Logan, fucker's always serious, can't say that I blame him, dealing with this fuckery.

"Right, this Stockton guy was in bed with the Porters we knew that already, but did you know that one of the Porters has the ear of one of our past presidents, anyone wanna take a guess as to which one?"

"Fuck, the fuck up?"
"You guessed it Law. Apparently while the rest of the world is under the impression that these fucks were after oil and other natural resources they had something more lucrative on the side. I'm guessing from all the silence that you already knew all this as well. I guess the big news then is that this desert guy whoever the fuck is headed stateside."

"How does your guy know this?" That sounded like Connor but what the fuck do I know?
"I'm guessing you don't know much about old man Mallory, you don't ask those kinda questions unless you wanna get dead."

"When?"
"He didn't say, only that they were plans being made."
"If this is true then we'd better get to work boys, he wouldn't risk coming here if it wasn't important, there has got to be something else going on that we haven't found yet. I can't see him coming here behind this shit."

"I say we end all the fucks and be done with it, Mallory gave me the names of two guys that might be able to help, maybe you know them."

"Who are they?"

"Mancini, he's some kinda spook outta New York very hush-hush and the other one's closer to our neck of the woods a Gideon Thorpe."

"Never heard of them. Creed you're pretty quiet, what's up?"

"Well Law, I know of Mancini and heard of Thorpe. If either of these two are coming onboard then Logan's right, the shit's about to hit the fan. Mancini is a dangerous fuck and Thorpe, well he's not one you wanna play with. They both have experience dealing with trafficking rings, that's how our paths crossed in the past."

"I'm with Con, that demented fuck isn't coming here because of child trafficking, that shit's child's play to a fuck like him. I say we follow Lyon's suggestion and start ending these fucks." That's my boy Ty. I knew I could count on him to have his head on straight.

"Hold it, we need to check this Intel, no offense to you or your friend, but if The Fox was heading this way don't you think we would've heard something?"

"No offense but do you think these conniving fucks will tell you the truth? I don't know who you've got on your end, but from everything I've heard so far, there's more shit being held back from you boys than what's being shared. Like I said before, I'm not beholden to any organization and I barely tolerate the laws that we have here since they change the shits as they go. I don't give a fuck who did what to who, all I want is the motherfucker that put my little girl in that book."

"We all want that Colton, but like we told you before, this thing is more intricate than the surface and your Intel if it's correct just proved it. This is a dangerous motherfucker no doubt and he has the money and the reach to make shit happen. My girl was in there too and believe me I wanna hop on a plane and go put one in the fuck myself, but they're others who need us and they need us to keep our heads and do this thing the right way."

"I hear you Cord and I didn't forget that you got a dog in this fight. I didn't forget that all of you have a stake in this. But you boys, including you Law and you Creed, have had that military training and forgive me for saying it, but I've never been on that leash. I don't care if I have to walk across the fucking Euphrates to get to this fuck I'd do it to keep my family safe. Creed, since you're the only one who knows these two boys that Mallory mentioned what do you think? You think it would help if we reached out?"

"It couldn't hurt, I'll have to find Mancini though, he's never in one place too long. I tell you what, I'm sick a this shit. Seems like the more we dig the more shit we unearth and we're still no closer to finding out the whys behind this thing. I haven't shared any of this shit with my girl, but she's starting to get suspicious on account of I won't even let her cross the door without someone on her."

For some fucked up reason, Char's words rang through my head just then. I might scoff at her shit and the fact that I have no idea how that shit works scares the shit outta me, but she's always on the money. Creed sounded like he was at the end of his rope and I imagined the others weren't far behind. "Uh, what're you boys doing for the holidays?"

"Say what now? Lyon you domesticated fuck, what're you talking about?"

Yeah, I'm domesticated but when we were at his place, his girl had him running in circles. "Law, you know every year we have the big shindig what's a couple more mouths?" What the fuck am I doing? "That goes for you boys too, you should bring out the wives get out of dodge for a few days. There's more than enough room here and at my folks we can all spread out. And if you boys ride your rig out then we can hook it up."

"Fuck Lo, we forgot the holidays we've been so busy focusing on this bullshit we dropped the ball."
"Don't panic Zak, it's weeks away."
"Fuck that Lo, what about baby Zak? We gotta get her Santa's list how the fuck do we do that? We gotta get on that shit like now."

I laughed my ass off at Ty and his rumblings while his brothers ribbed him to death. "We forgot something else, there're four pregnant women in this crew, and Law's is breeding too, y'all sure these girls are up to taking this trip?"

"I don't see why not Quinn. They made it a month or so ago, plus we can always fly out. What do you think Lo?" That was the first time Devon spoke since we got started. That boy reminds me of someone with his silent shit, I don't trust it one fuck. Fucker's probably the deadliest one of the bunch.

They talked it out while I sat there wondering what the fuck had happened to my life. It was passing strange to be discussing holiday plans and fuckery in the middle of a shit storm, but seems that's way we were going. "One thing boys, we don't discuss this shit while you're here, not unless we're one hundred percent sure there're no ears around. My family are heavy into this Xmas shit, I don't want anything fucking that up."

"Lyon, your word that you won't move on this until we've done some searching."
"I don't make promises, but I can tell you that if those fucks don't make a move towards me I'll hold off. You fucks take too long though who knows." Logan didn't seem too pleased with that but he'll have to deal, he ain't my damn team leader.

In the end, they said they'd get back after discussing things with their women and I went to tell Kat that we might be having about twenty more mouths to feed in a week. I was already regretting that shit.

What the fuck was I supposed to do with these fucks if they show up here?

Chapter 13
Lyon
***

"Kat, what the hell is all that shit you got around the house, and why the fuck does it feel like I haven't seen you in a week?" Even as I spoke she was bustling in and out of the room. She knows I hate it when she ignores me and she's been doing that shit for the last few days, ever since I got the call that the guys were coming for the holidays.

Elena was in her element, she likes nothing more than having a horde to feed and fuss over. Kat had invited that boys people to my damn house as well and my kids were losing their fucking minds because the living room looked like the backroom of a toy store with all the damn gifts under the humongous tree I'd had to cut down.

"The only time I see you anymore is when it's time for bed. You're always puttering around here, cut that shit out." She gave me one of her looks. " Who was it that invited overnight guests huh? Who was it

that told me the week before Xmas that we
had more people coming?"

She had a point but that didn't mean I
liked this shit. "Where's the baby?"
"He's asleep I just put him down why?" I
walked over to the corner where she keeps
the traveling crib. She's been keeping the
baby in here with us under the guise of
having him close so she could hear him but I
knew it was because he was the last one and
she was trying to get all the mothering in
that she could.

I bent down and picked him up
ignoring her hissing behind me. He smelt
like a baby, and I felt that jump in my heart I
always get when I sniff one of my kids. "I
think we need another one Kat." Her eyes
widened and she took a step back like she
expected me to jump on her right then and
there.

"Colton, are you nuts? You just got
through telling me two days ago that we
shouldn't have had the ones we have and
now…"
"Girls, Kat it's your damn daughters that are
putting me in the grave. But look at him,
he's growing up so fast don't you want
another one?" Her eyes got all soft and she

rubbed her legs together. I knew I had her, just needed to reel her in.

"Come on babe, imagine all the fun we're gonna have trying." I walked over and rubbed my hand between her legs until she was wet, then I sucked her tongue into my mouth and it was a done deal.

"Oh alright, but I don't want to hear any complaints if we end up with another girl." Zinger, she knew damn well she didn't want one either, that damn Catalina is about all we can handle. She's been running around here like a nut since we told her there were new people coming. Probably saw them as guinea pigs.

***

Today was the day the boys were coming to town. There weren't that many preparations to be made as far as safety. No one here had messed with me and mine in a long time, but still, I had the boys do a perimeter run, you never know. This fucking holiday tends to bring out the crazies or some fuck.

I had a fuckload of shit to do before they got here. Our yearly charity run which my kids had joined once they were old enough, and all the last minute shit Kat and Elena were gonna have me doing. The madness had already started with Kat and her mother in law taking over my kitchen. I tried to avoid Char who kept giving me secret smiles like she knew some fuck I didn't.

"Elena, where's your husband?" She was busy stirring something while her granddaughter, my Caitie bear, watched. It's a sight I've seen every year since she was born, one that still brings a tingle to my heart and one I won't be giving up anytime soon.

"He had something to do at the hospital but he should be here when your little friends show up. Char tells me they're all rather…robust."
"Why the hell are you blushing ma and how can Glenda the witch tell you anything when she's never seen these boys before?"

"Oh son, don't be such a prude and you know very well how she knows." She gave me the 'Colton is stupid' look while my daughter pretended she wasn't hearing shit and my wife hummed carols as she flitted around the room.

"Kat, come here a minute."

"Oh dear, I know that tone, whatever it is, she's done. You're gonna have to deal with it later son. We have lots to do and not nearly enough time, what with you springing a hundred extra people on us last minute." That's Elena, queen of exaggeration. "Kat, now."

She huffed her ass across the room. I notice she always gets a little more spunky when her meddling ass mother in law is around, add her own mother to the mix and I have a coup on my hand. "You're not wearing that thing whatever it is you have on when the others get here, go change."

She looked down at herself and even though I'd said it as quietly as possible the room's other occupants still rolled their eyes at me. "Colton what's wrong with what I have on?" She spread her arms out at her sides and the damn button down shirt tightened across her ample tits.

"Get it off and put something over those tights things, they show off too much of your ass."
"What should she wear son, you got burlap somewhere? Maybe we can whip her up a gunnysack right quick." They all thought that shit was funny. "And you think she's

moving in here in a few years?" I whispered that shit in my wife's ear because it was too damn close to the holiday to deal with their shit.

"Colton, behave we've already settled that issue, now why don't you go choose something for me to wear and I'll be right up in a minute to put it on?" Yeah right, she thinks I'm too preoccupied to remember my own name. "Katarina do I look like I'm playing with you? If you want me to choose something for you to wear I can."

She had enough sense to know what that shit meant and went up to change. I didn't give a fuck about the snickers from the other women in the room when I turned to follow her. Nosy fucks.

I cornered her to the bedroom after watching her ass twitch all the way up the stairs. "Here let me help you." I went after her top first sending buttons flying across the room.
"Colton we can't…" She tried covering her tits in the half bra she wore but the die had already been cast and my boy was on the rise.

"If you didn't want to get fucked you shouldn't have worn that." I took her down and got my mouth on her tit and my hand between her legs. There's no feeling like stealing the pussy with a house full of people. I had to stuff Kat's damn mouth while I drilled her from behind hard and sweet.

Her pussy gripped me like a glove as she pushed her ass back into my strokes, spreading her legs for me. I fingered her clit and marked her neck while the sap rose in my balls. "I'm cumming baby you there?"

"Uh-huh." I can still make her voice go weak. Her pussy quivered around my cock and she scratched the sheets as I sped up my pounding strokes into her, sending my dick deep into her belly. I tried not to fuck with her hair when I held her head down in the pillow as I offloaded about a pint of jizz in her pussy.

I let the last drop drip into her before pulling out and tapping my pierced cock head onto her ass crack. I moved back and pulled her panties back up her legs. "Don't clean up, I want my scent on you when those boys get here, don't want any misunderstandings."

"Colton seriously? Aren't these people your friends?" She went to dig through her clothes in the closet while I tried to catch my breath on the bed. Her ass did look too good in those things and I knew it was because she was still carrying some extra from when she was breeding with Cody. I dare not say that shit though or she'd get to starving her ass or some fuck to lose weight and I hate that shit. "I don't care Kat, it's a man thing don't question it."

I tongue fucked her mouth before leaving her to figure out her wardrobe. "By the way, don't forget to have the kids ready in twenty. We have to be at the hospital an hour ago."

"They'll be ready, oh Colt can you please have a talk with Catalina? She's so excited about the others coming that I'm afraid of what she might do."
"Afraid someone else might figure out she's fucking nuts?"
"COLTON." Damn she likes to yell.

To keep her happy, I did go in search of the mad scientist but for once she was behaving. "Look daddy, isn't this pretty? Mom said I look like a princess." She was wearing some flowery thing with ribbons and shit in her hair and she did look like your average five year old the way she sat there like she was waiting patiently for the festivities to start. Too bad for her ass I don't trust her.

"Where're your brothers?" They're usually her targets of choice and it was only a few weeks ago that I had to save poor Aiden from one of her concoctions that once thrown down the sink had smoked and fumed and given off the most awful odor in creation.

"They're around somewhere, but daddy you didn't say, isn't my dress pretty?" "It's beautiful kid, come give your old man a hug." She got a pained look on her face and I knew why five seconds later when I heard all three of her brothers trampling down the stairs calling for their mother at the top of their lungs. It could have something to do with the many keys under her ass when she got up from the corner of the couch where she'd been sitting.

"What did they do to you?" I wasn't gonna laugh, Kat says that only encourages her, not that the kid needs any encouragement, she's a one man army and just like her old man, she don't give a fuck.

"They won't let me play."
"Do you really wanna play in your pretty clothes?"

"The boys are playing in theirs why can't I? it's not fair daddy. Caitie doesn't play with me she's too old and the boys say I'm just a girl." I tried explaining that shit to her until she got a strange light in her eyes before grabbing her contraband and trying to make a run for it. "I know, I'll play with Cody…"

"Hold it." I had to talk her out of using her brother as a science project, the shit she had in mind would land us all in jail. Where the fuck does she come up with this shit? "Catalina, your brother is not a doll, he hurts just as you do. You cannot pin his eyes back to see how they work." What the fuck? Who thinks of this shit? I'm gonna have to remember to tell Kat not to leave those two alone.

***

They started trickling in early evening, first Law and his crew, followed by Creed and his. By the time the SEALs showed up, I was afraid the neighbors were gonna call out the National Guard. Mallory wasn't coming tonight. He had a kid with a fever so Kat and I would have to make a run out to their place after the holidays if things didn't change by tomorrow.

We made a sight in the upscale neighborhood with its preppy shit. I could just imagine the curtains being pulled back and the calls to nine-one- one. The SEALs had flown in and rented two SUVs and by the time my whole crew showed up the front of my house looked like a hoedown.

Kat and Elena had gone all out to make the houses ready and make sure there was more than enough room for everyone so nobody had to stay at a hotel. Elena was getting the most of it since she had more available space, but the way things were looking the women were all bunking in my damn living room.

I don't know what it is about females, but they gravitate towards each other like bees to their queen, add a couple pregnancies to the mix and men become damn near nonexistent. At least Kat had a smile on her face as she made the rounds making sure her new guests were comfortable.

"Well Lyon, we made it." Law sidled up to me in the middle of the mayhem that was taking place in my living room. "I'm glad you came." I was surprised to realize that was true, though my house looks like an outlaw crew had overrun it.

People were spread out from the backyard to the driveway. Somebody had turned on the stereo and Xmas carols were piping through the speaker system, and the women were passing around trays of food and drinks.

The house felt like it was supposed to the night before Xmas, light and happy. It was enlightening to see that I wasn't the only husband who had lost his damn mind. The way these boys hovered around their women, taking care of their every need, you'd think no one had ever carried a child before.

The kids were in their element, even my boys who were usually stoic little fucks were having the time of their lives showing off their riding skills. I kept my eye on Catalina as she flitted from room to room. She had everyone fooled from the get. All the women were goo-goo over her and she had the men wrapped around her little finger.

I figure they were all watching her and imagining what their little angels might be when they finally got here, if they only knew. I knew I was the one who'd said no shoptalk but by the time the women were settled I was making eye contact with the guys to follow me outside. I could see that though they were willing to put shit aside for their women's sake, they wanted to get shit moving.

Chapter 14
Kat
***

Once everyone was settled and my guests were comfortable, I set myself to spying. I'd never heard about most of these people before, and found it strange that they were here with Law, which could only mean that they were involved somehow in whatever it was that was giving Colton fits since his visit to Law's.

I'd been plotting since the moment he told me that they were coming, and though I was more than happy to have them, that joy was twofold. I wanted answers, and since I knew none of the men were going to be forthcoming, I knew just where to get them.

Colton wasn't being his usual gruff self whenever there was anything carrying testosterone in my vicinity, so I knew that he was preoccupied, the only thing that would do that in my opinion, was if this thing whatever it was, had to do with one of us, even one of the kids.

I know him very well he forgets that I was there when that crazy girl was after me years ago, and the way he'd reacted. If I were the one in danger, I'd be strapped into a chair somewhere with an armed guard on twenty-four hour duty. That could only mean one thing, it was one of the kids, but try as I might I couldn't put it together.

He's been keeping a close watch on Caitlin since that night, even going so far as to have someone posted outside the school while she was there, but I'd put it down to the thing with Todd and had even gone so far as to tease him about it. The thought that she might be in danger made my stomach hurt, but I didn't want to jump to conclusions.

I kept things light and played the hostess while the men were inside, but all the while I was biding my time, sizing up the women. I knew from little snippets here and there that these women were at Law's place when Colt went there, and that's where they'd met. But I also gathered that they didn't know much more than I did. These men; still, they were close to the action and I know that if they were anything like me, they must know something.

"So you're all planning weddings? That must be stressful with all that the guys have going on." I started in as soon as I saw Colt leading the guys outside. Colt was outside and the kids were off showing baby Zakira around. I didn't miss the looks that passed between them, or the way they all checked to see where their men were same as I had.

"I know one thing, if they don't get it taken care of come May I'm gonna go hunt these fools down myself." Gabriella folded her legs and took a sip of her ginger ale while the others snickered. "Yeah, and Logan would skin you alive, you're in enough trouble as it is from the last stunt. Me, I'm not about to step on Zak's toes anytime soon, he's already acting like a wounded bear and he's only gotten worse since we came back from Law's."

"Nice little getaway my butt; that's what they tried to sell us, that the trip out to Law's was just to get away. Then the first night we were there they disappeared." Dani rolled her eyes and sniffed. I knew I liked these women. They might look like southern belles and runway models, but they weren't stupid.

"Wait, go hunt who down?" There was dead silence as the women all exchanged looks before sizing me up themselves. I didn't feel anyway, didn't take it personally, after all, they didn't know me from Adam, but it was obvious they knew something and if me, and my family were involved I wanted in.

"Look ladies, I know we've just met and you have no reason to trust me, but our husbands are obviously working on something together and you know some if not all of it. My house has been an armed camp for the last month or so and I'd like to know why. So if there's anything you can tell me…"

"If Ty knew we were talking about this he'd have a fit, but I'm with the rest of you. How much do you know Katarina?" Victoria-Lyn was the most forward of the bunch though a little reserved. Vanessa was like a mother hen watching out for the rest of them. Even from her seat in the chair it was obvious she was on alert, probably some kind of military training.

Dani and Gaby played the debutante role very well, but they weren't fooling me, these women were smart, they had to be with the men they were marrying, they'd need to know how to hold their own. Dana Sue, Ginger Lee, Melissa, Illyana and Suzette seemed a little rough around the edges, like they'd seen more than the others. I knew they were from Law's place and though I didn't know too much about the goings on there, I knew that he'd seen some trouble not too long ago with the loss of his family.

Jessie if I remember correctly was Creed's wife, she seemed young, and bore a slight resemblance to me at that age in her behavior and mannerisms. I liked them all, but there was something about her that touched me. She gave off this aura of innocence that made you want to protect her from the big bad world.

And then there was Susie, the youngest of the bunch. It was cute the way her eyes followed the muscle bound SEAL and the way he kept her in his sights at all times. The others were always strategically placed near their women when in the same room, kinda like Colt, and it was good to see that I wasn't the only one married to a nut.

"I know that Colton left here one day to visit a friend and came back and put us all under lock and key. For a good week I was expecting I don't know what, but I do know he's been trying really hard to act like everything's okay when I know it ain't and his answer for everything is 'it's nothing for you to worry about baby." We all had a good laugh at my impersonation of Mr. Lyon.

"Oh he's one of those too is he? They're all the same. Law just tells me not to worry my pretty little head about anything like that's all that's needed." Dana Sue glared towards the French doors where we could see the men standing around in deep conversation.

"Sounds like Clay, but ladies, as an author I do a lot of observing and snooping around and I make no excuses for it. I can tell you that Clay has been working overtime on something." Ginger looked pensive as she sat back in her chair and tapped her fingers on her knee.

"I didn't say anything before because I wasn't sure, but mom said something was going on before the guys snatched her. Some guy from Georgia was coming, he's related to my grandfather but he's some big shot or something. I heard Brandon mention that guy's name after everyone came to visit."

"Illyana you're holding out?"
"No Ginger, I just didn't think it meant anything at the time. We were all just worried about Jess remember? And the guys were being so hush-hush about everything…"

"When aren't they being that way? So we're all agreed that something's up and all our guys are involved. What was the name Illyana?" Melissa had trouble written all over her face, the kind of fun type that would keep you in the best kind of mischief.

"Stanton, Stockton, one of those I think." The girls from Georgia went on high alert and you could feel the tension in the room go up a few degrees. "What? Who is he?" The rest of us looked towards them as they became restless.

"Okay maybe we should start at the beginning. The guys don't know we know this so keep it between us promise? I don't want to deal with Connor and his craziness. Ever since I told him about the baby he's been like a raving lunatic, I'm lucky I'm allowed to step out the front door these days." The conversation turned to the craziness that ensues when one of our men hear the word pregnant.

"Okay Dani, we all know our boys are way past gone in the head, now what do you know?" Gaby moved to the edge of her seat as the rest of us waited with baited breath.

"Now understand, I only know bits and pieces, and you guys know most of what I know, but maybe we all know enough to piece this mess together. When the guys first moved to town there were whispers about stuff going on down by the water at night. No one ever had any real evidence to support anything, but after the guys came, I noticed at night that Con and the others would go down there to stake out the place."

"Then Gaby there was that night you and I went looking and dragged Vanessa with us and those guys almost nabbed us. They were military, Vanessa you told us about the woman who used to work for me, and dragging her back but we never saw her, so we assumed that she was part of whatever was going on.

Then there's Stockton, that's Victoria-Lynn's story." Our attention turned to Vicky who had been quiet ever since the name came up. She cleared her throat and looked uncomfortable before she started.

"When he was working me over in that room he kept asking me about Ty. I thought he'd somehow found out that I was in love with Ty and was just jealous because I wouldn't give him the time of day. It was only after that I kinda thought it might be something else. You all know how tight lipped these guys are, but I've heard bits and pieces which I've shared with my sisters. Stockton is involved in some kind of trafficking deal, I don't know what, drugs maybe, but I have no proof."

"I don't know, drugs, don't do it for me."
"Well what do you suggest Vanessa?"
"I don't know, but the other night the guys were in my kitchen. They thought I was asleep, but I had to get up to check on the baby since she's been teething and I heard something." She stopped short and checked the French doors where the men were still visible."

"Well don't leave us in suspense, what did you hear?" Gaby knocked her leg with hers. "I heard a name, one I've never heard outside a closed room with people who have the highest security clearance. Mancini."

"Who is he?"

"Not many people know, but I do know if our boys are playing around with him, then whatever is going on here is bigger than drugs."

"I'm almost sorry I asked, all this talk is only make me more paranoid, what are we going to do?" I'm not sure what I'd been expecting them to say, but all this talk was making me more nervous that my Colt might be involved in something that could get him hurt or worse.

Once we realized that each of us had little bits and pieces and when added together came up with a whole, the picture started to come into focus, but there were still big gaping holes needing to be filled.

It was amazing even with the subject matter, how easy it was for all of us to sit around like this, like old friends. Elena wasn't here she'd only stayed around long enough to meet everyone and welcome them ahead of the big day.

I hadn't shared my suspicions with her I didn't have anything to share. I think Colton had shared what was going on with his father and mine because of all the secret meets in the study. Of course us little old ladies were too soft to get involved. Now I had to find a way to put all this new info to good use.

"I don't know about you ladies, but I'm thinking we need to keep in touch. It's blatantly obvious that if we want to know what's going on with these men of ours that we're gonna have to be sneaky about it. So what do you say we keep our ears to the ground and see if we can finish this puzzle."

"Sounds good to me Katarina, we already exchanged numbers and emails with Dana Sue and the others when we visited a few weeks ago, we'll be sure and do the same before we leave."

"Thanks Vanessa that sounds like a great plan. Oh crap Colt's watching, let's change the subject."

Chapter 15
Lyon
***

"How much do your women know about this little situation we're dealing with?"

"Nothing why?" Logan turned to look in the same direction I was, a direct view into the great room where the women had gathered. "Look at them in there. I haven't heard any laughter coming from in there, no one's pulling anyone's hair so they're not fighting, but they're all very engrossed in whatever's going on. And look there, the body language just changed as soon as my wife noticed me looking."

"There's no way they know." I had everyone's attention now for a different reason. We'd all been kicking around ideas about the best move to make and getting nowhere because the SEALs were on some waiting shit. Now we had another problem on our hands.

"I know a way to find out what they know." I twisted my lips and made the call I use on special occasions, it's a call only one person knows. She came running a few seconds later, all smiles and innocence. Her mother had put a bow in her hair and done some shit to her curls that made them shine in the moonlight. She looked like a fairytale or some fuck, but I know better.

"Come here Catalina." She was a little shy with all the men around but she came. "What's your mother up to in there?" Yes I know it's fucked that I use my kid this way, but she's better than some of the guys on my payroll at this shit. She gave me a suspicious look at first, like she thought I was trying to trap her since I've been telling her forever about listening in at doors and shit. I guess she decided I was on the up and up, fucking kid.

She looked around at the others before crooking her finger at me. I walked a few steps away until we were out of earshot. "I didn't hear everything because I had to lose the others." Who the fuck is this kid? "But they were saying something about the traffic and some of the ladies got into trouble for going to the water and the bad man almost got them." She took a breath and creased her brow in concentration.

"One of the pretty ladies got work from Stockton, oh and Micini whoever that is." She looked up at me in expectation the little sneak. I could only look at her in amazement. It was on the tip of my tongue to scold her for listening to other people's shit again but that would be hypocritical. I also knew there was no point in telling her not to do that shit because she wouldn't listen no how, just like her damn mother. "Catalina why were you listening in on their conversation?"

"Nobody tells me anything." Like she's a hundred years old. "Go play with the others and no more snooping or I'll ground you again." She rolled her eyes because she knew I was full of shit, we have the weirdest fucking relationship. I'm sure some shrink would have a field day with it, but it works for us.

"Daddy did you remember to tell Santa about my chemistry set?" Here comes the shakedown, maybe she'd become a politician and save my ass bond money because sure as fuck she's gonna be a danger to society.
"Yeah I told the fat fu…er, yeah he knows." She skipped her little ass back inside and I went back to the guys.

"They know."
"What do you mean they know, who told them? They can't know. We've been very careful about that. Davey did you let anything slip to your sister?" Logan turned to the kid that was always in their shadow. He shook his head with a frown on his face.

"How can I tell her anything when you guys keep me pretty much outta the loop?" I would feel sorry for him, if I hadn't caught him eyeing my Caitie bear earlier when they first arrived. She didn't even so much as blink in his direction thank fuck, I'd hate to have to hurt the kid. Then again her reaction posed another problem. She was so caught up in Todd the fuck, she didn't even see other boys when they were standing in front of her giving off signals. That's for another time though, right now I have to figure out what my wife and her new friends were up to.

"How much do you think they know, and how does your kid know?"
"My kid would outdo any Russian spy, she's female, she's young and adorable so most people don't pay too much mind to her, that's part of her ammo. The other part is listening in at doors and shit, that's why I said no talking shop, you never know when she's around with her shit."

The SEALs looked after the door where she'd disappeared like they were thinking of recruiting her. Crazy fucks. "Damn I wonder if baby Zak is gonna do shit like that."
"With her mother's genes she'd probably be worst Ty. Lyon what did your kid say, how much do they know?" Zak asked me the question again.

"Well, they know about the trafficking, and they have the name Mancini." I wasn't sure how I felt about Kat knowing about this shit, at least Caitie bear's name hadn't come up; if it had Catalina would've told me. Still they knew more than enough to make trouble for my ass, because women always want to be in the mix, I know mine does. If she has reinforcements, women feeding her shit I want kept secret, who knows.

"This doesn't make sense, how can they know?"
"They're comparing notes." Cord had his eyes glued to the youngest one in the fold.
"What notes, how can they know anything? Dana Sue spent the last month or so puking up her guts every hour on the hour, when did she have time to be getting into my shit?

Kyle it's your damn wife, she's the only one who'd snoop into this shit."

"Hold it, don't forget Ginger, she does that snooping shit for a living, and Brand your woman might've heard some shit while she was up there with her people, or her mother could've told her." Now we were the ones trying to figure shit out.

"It doesn't matter, the cat's out of the bag, now we do damage control. Who's gonna go in there and put the fear in them? I don't know about yours, but mine don't listen for shit and if she thinks she can help me with this she'd try. That is not gonna happen." Fucking Kat couldn't give me one day of peace.

"Well Lyon, since it's your house I say you get to do the honors." Connor grinned but I could tell he wasn't too pleased by this turn of events either. From what I gathered, all the women in there except mine and the youngest one were breeding. If these boys were anything like me, and I was beginning to suspect they were when it came to their women at least, that wasn't gonna go over too well. A man would go to any lengths to protect his woman and unborn child.

"Scared of them are you?"

"You have no idea." He clapped me on the shoulder as we made our way towards the house. My boys, the ones who go on certain runs with me, had been brought up to speed. Tomorrow Mallory would be here if his kid was doing better and I'll let him in on whatever he didn't already know.

***

Inside the talk had turned to babies, but the tension was still thick in the air. "Kat, what were you talking about earlier? And before you answer, your daughter already told me."

"Dammit Colton you put her up to it." She wasn't looking too happy the little sneak. Her friends had looks of confusion on their faces until I told them what had happened.

"We know nothing, just girls sitting around getting to know each other." The one named Gabriella sat back and crossed her legs and arms with the most innocent look on her face. Logan walked over and leaned over to whisper something in her ear that made her twitchy.

"Quit it Logan we weren't doing anything wrong."

"Who told you about the trafficking?" He stood back and folded his arms like a general but the look she gave him said she wasn't scared. "Duh, there were rumors around town before you guys showed up, and you spend an awful lot of time down there snooping around, and let's not forget Dani and Nessa and I…"

"Yes I remember, and I would hope that that one experience would've taught you to stay out of it. How many times must I tell you?" She was out of her chair and in his face before he could get the words out. "Listen you, these fools whoever they are-are interfering with the most important day of my life. I can't even go get my nails done anymore because you have me under lock and key. It wouldn't take a genius to figure out something is going on Logan, and unless you think I'm a brainless twit it only stands to reason I'm gonna go searching for answers…"

"Sit down." She pouted but found her ass in her chair. I wonder if he'd teach me that trick. Fifteen years and counting and I still can't bring Kat's little ass to heel. He walked around the room with his arms behind his back and a look on his face. I see why the others let him take point he has leader pouring off him in spades.

I held my peace for now. I'll deal with Kat's ass later behind closed doors. I guess I can't fault her, or any of them for wanting to know what was taking up so much of their man's time, but I didn't want her anywhere near this shit. Not because I didn't want her knowing what I'd done in the desert all those years ago, but because I'd made a promise, a promise to her. That nothing like this would ever touch her again, and I mean to keep that promise.

The room looked like a standoff, men on one side, women on the other and these girls looked ready to throw down. I guess they were shoring each other up, strength in numbers or some shit. Whatever Logan was coming with had better be good.

"Fine, so you all know some but not all of what's going on, what do you plan to do with this knowledge?" Their eyes opened wide and the Georgia peaches looked at each other like 'what the fuck?' I wasn't sure myself, but if these men were anything like me when it came to dealing with my nosy ass hardheaded woman, I was waiting for the other shoe to drop.

"No one?" Damn, he does leashed cool like a pro.

"Well since you're asking, we'd like to know more about why our lives have been turned upside down. If we're in some kind of danger it's only fair that we know what's going on." Dani spoke up but she kept taking sneak peeks at Connor, sweet, she's making sure she doesn't overstep.

I took each one's measure as they spoke their piece, gauging how much they knew beyond what my little spy had told me. Logan had the floor. The others just stood back and listened as he grilled them like a paid interrogator. They teach these boys some serious shit in the navy because he was good.

"I guess there's no point in telling you lot to stay out of this, you've proven that you don't listen worth shit." He glared at his woman who pursed her lips and looked away. "So here's the deal and I'm sure every man here will back me up. Gabriella, you don't drop this shit I will march your little ass down to the courthouse and put my ring on your finger, there goes your big to-do."

She huffed and opened her mouth but he cut her off. I hope Kat was seeing this shit and taking notes hardheaded fuck. "Don't say one more word. I brought you here for a change of pace, to have a nice holiday with new friends. This man invited us into his home and what do you do? You bring this shit here, to these women."

"Hold it, she didn't bring anything to my home. If you'll excuse me, we don't know each other but I've been married to your twin for the better part of almost sixteen years and I know when I'm being played. We're not backing down, we wanna know what's going on, why all the secrecy and high security." That's my wife she's been taking lessons from fucking Elena again.

Logan shrugged his shoulders with a smirk. "Well boys I tried." Dammit that means I still had work to do, fucking Kat. There were more glares going around the room being ignored before we headed back out. "Dude they played you in there, those women are not easy. I guess they have to be that way to put up with you goons huh."

Jared the ass always has something smart to say. I guess he expects us all to leave our balls at home with the wife like he does. "No, they didn't. We now know what they know and it's not much. The trafficking thing like my delightful fiancé said, was a rumor long before we came on the scene.

They've been playing the guessing game since we nabbed the two assholes on the waterfront and we have to surmise that Vanessa told them about grabbing Dani's ex employee. Other than that they know nothing." Damn Logan's good.

"You're forgetting one thing, they got Mancini's name according to the kid."
"Yeah but Creed said no one knows much about him Law."
"Vanessa might, she had clearance; if this guy is on anyone's radar she might've heard something."
"Well fuck Zak."

"No need to panic Ty, that just means we stem the flow."
"And how do you propose we do that Con?"
"By talking to our women and letting them know the consequences if they disobey us on this shit, by letting them know that this is not child's play and it is definitely nothing for women to get mixed up in."

"Good luck with that shit, if they're anything like my bloodhound, then they won't quit until they get what they want and from the looks of them, they've banded together. So unless you plan on monitoring their every move I suggest you come up with another plan." And tomorrow we have

Elena and fucking Char coming, more reinforcements.

"Seriously, what the fuck are you all on? Since when do we let women dictate to us?"
"What's your big suggestion Creed?"
"Well Law, I just tell Babygirl how shit's gonna be and that's that, she better not be getting mixed up in this shit, I don't want her knowing anything about that fucking book."

"You fucks are all newbies." I shook my head as they turned to look at me. "You have only two options when it comes to dealing with these women, you give them fucked up info or you make damn sure they stay put. It's getting late and I have to go deal with my pain in the ass and see how much she got from yours because I know for damn sure she didn't get anything from me."

Chapter 16
Lyon
***

Part of the crew headed to Elena's while the others stayed here. I had my guys give them an escort though I was sure they didn't need one, but it was courtesy. "You, upstairs." I'd waited until she said her goodbyes to all her little friends and locked up.

"Don't you start, you've been holding out on me and that's not part of the marriage code." She rewrites that shit every chance she gets.
"Feeling brave are you?" We rounded up the kids and packed them off to bed after fighting with Catalina about waiting up for the fat fuck. The baby was the last one we checked on before heading for bed.

It was well past midnight and tomorrow was going to be a long one. "So, what was it that you were trying to find out?" She started getting twitchy as we got undressed for bed. I think my tones be tipping her off or some shit, I guess it comes with years of marriage.

I have no issue with her snooping-she's a female-it's in the genes or some fuck. But what I do mind is that she went behind my back. I hadn't taken her to task for doing it with Law, things were too hot then, but this, no excuse.

"Did you ask me what was going on? I asked you a question, I expect an answer."
"Colton…" One lifted brow was all it took to get her talking.
"Yes I did."
"And what did I say?"
"You said it was nothing but I know…"
"Hey." Her voice had gone up one too many octaves there and since she was already teetering on the brink of an ass whipping I was trying to save her seeing that it was the fucking holidays and we had company.

"I told you to leave it alone, so you decided to go elsewhere for answers, what does that sound like to you Kat?" Of course she pretended great interest in folding her clothes and putting them in the hamper before giving me an answer.

"We were just talking, it's not like we went out trying to hunt these people down ourselves. We're not children you know, we have just as much right to know what's going on in our lives, in your lives…" I listened to her rant and rave as I got undressed myself and climbed into bed. I waited until she was close to winding down.

"You done? Get over here." If she thought I was gonna waste my breath with her hardheaded ass she was wrong. I talk long enough to be clear on the infraction and then I act. I opened the top drawer of the nightstand and took out what I needed. When she saw the lineup her voice started cracking up but it was too late.

It wasn't that she'd disobeyed so much as she'd shown our hand in front of the others. I don't know how those boys deal with their women and it's none of my concern. But for my wife to pump our guests for information after I'd invited them to our home was a big fucking no-no.

I'm sure her mind wouldn't see it that way, fucking female. But if a man can't control his home he can't handle shit else and no one will respect him. She was halfway to the door by the time I finished tying the last rope to the four corners of the bed.

"Get your ass back here." I didn't turn to make sure she was obeying me, I knew her ass better do what I said. I hate doing this shit to her, it had been a while since we've been here, but this shit we were dealing with was heading south fast and I didn't want her little ass nowhere near it.

She sat down hard on the bed with a heavy dose of attitude, but she knew better than to open her mouth. The tears had started but I ignored them, too bad for her, she'd brought this shit on herself. "Lay down." I helped her into the middle of the bed and tied her arms before gagging her.

After I was sure her ties were snug, I retrieved the leg spreader for the real fun. She made noises around the ball gag but I was already in cold mode. I couldn't hear shit. I spread her legs open and kept them in the air. Next came the belt. She screamed bloody murder when the first lash landed on her inner thigh, and was weeping uncontrollably by the tenth.

She hadn't stopped fighting against her restraints though, so my work was far from done. Next I went after her clit with the vibrator while fingering her pussy, pulling out each time I felt the little tremors that signaled her orgasm.

I kept that up for a good half an hour until I thought she'd had enough. I removed the leg spreader, tied her legs to the bed and walked out. "Good night."

***

She was pissed beyond measure by the time I released her early the next morning. "Wait, I didn't tell you to move." She laid back on the bed and I took a few to clear my head before leaning over her. "Leave it." I didn't need to say anymore than that for her to get my meaning.

She'll never know the fear that went through me when the guys and I headed back outside and the SEALs let the rest of us in on what we were dealing with. The lengths some of the people involved would go to. The thought of her getting close to that shit sent fear down my spine.

"You can get up now, we have company. If I see one pout today I'm not gonna be happy." I headed for the shower while she went to get the baby who was starting to fuss. The damn temp in the room was sub zero, merry fucking Xmas to me.

My place looked like a biker's convention by the time all our guests showed up. This was supposed to be an all day thing with people in and out. We'd done the charity rounds the day before so all I had to do today was keep the ice bucket full and the beer cold.

My mom showed up early to help my wife who was still not speaking to me and I noticed the other women weren't looking too happy either, and the men had about the same look as I did. I guess a lot had been said and done behind closed doors last night after everyone went to bed. Hopefully the shit worked because it would only take one rogue female to fuck our shit up.

"Colton, what did you do to my daughter in law?"
"I have no idea of what you speak Elena." She tried to corner me in the kitchen while she was reloading on eggs. "Well she's not her usual self and I know the only thing that can do that is you since my grandkids all seem cheerful and gay."

"Why don't you get your eggs and quit harassing me ma." I was dodging

Char's ass again since she had a million and
one questions. I was surprised that she
hadn't told Elena or Kat about her hoodoo
shit. The next time she tried to corner me I
let her to ask her just that.

"Well Colton, thank you for my very
lovely Xmas gift."
"They're not here for you Char but I do have
a question. If you see what you claim to,
how come you haven't shared with your
posse?" Her whole attitude changed and she
looked around to make sure the coast was
clear.

"I try not to worry my friends
unnecessarily. If I thought for a second we
could do anything about the situation you
better believe I would've blown the whistle
by now. But not on this one."

"What is it that you see exactly?" It
must be the first time I'd taken her seriously,
the first time I'd ever asked her to explain.
That day when she saw whatever it was she
saw about Kat, I had felt it, the surety the
fear. It was then I had begun to give
credence to her many ramblings. Since then
I've steered clear.

"I see darkness, great darkness and
men with black souls. There's a lot of murky

water, death. But I do see an end to it, but there will be a lot of chaos surrounding the whole mess." I wonder what the others would think if I shared this little powwow with them? Probably that I'd lost my damn mind

"Thanks Char, now go behave yourself." I took five minutes to let her words sink in before joining the melee again. I don't know how the women did it, but there was a never -ending flow of food and drink, and the kids were on their best behavior.

By mid afternoon, Kat was over her snit but I noticed her conversation was all about babies and weddings. She might be playing it safe since I was in the room but I don't think so. After last night's little lesson, I was sure she'd keep her ass still, but I didn't fool myself that the shit would last longer than it took for the pain from her spanking to go away.

The phone rang on my hip and I answered without looking. "Lyon, Mancini here, I hear you're looking for me?" I snapped my fingers to get Law's attention and he alerted the others. "Are you there?"

"I'm here, trying to get to a secure location."

"No worries it's taken care of." I took the phone away from my ear and looked at it. Who the fuck? "Okay, well I have some others here who would like to hear what you have to say."

"The call's cleared for you, Lawton Daniels, Justice Creed and the SEALs no one else I don't care how close you are."

Well since this fuck knows so much…"You missed one."

"Mallory's not there he's got a sick kid." Fucking spook.

"Okay, we're all in. I'm going to speaker now." The noise outside the door was steady, but inside my study you could hear a pin drop.

"I did some digging into your situation. I don't know how much the SEALs have shared with the rest of you, but you're swimming in very murky waters." I felt a cold chill run down my spine. Those were almost exactly the words Char had said to me not too long ago.

"If you go after this, you better be sure you know what you're going into. They will come after your families, your friends and your businesses. Any and everything they can to stop you. The trafficking is only the tip of the iceberg, I have Intel that Khalil is on his way to the states but not for the reasons you may think."

"What's he after?"
"I'm not at liberty to share that at this time."
Fucking diplomat.
"Does that mean you don't know?"
"I always know." I like this fucker, never mince words.

"Mancini, Logan here, we already guessed that The Fox wasn't coming here behind this, so you're not telling us anything new here. I'm pretty sure you knew that already so what's the real reason for your call?"

There was a snicker and then throat clearing. "Look behind you gentlemen." We all turned to look at the door. "Catalina what are you doing in here?"
"I was here first daddy." She had a doll in her lap as she sat quietly in the corner. I had no idea if she was telling the truth or not, I'd stopped eyeballing her about an hour ago when it seemed like she was gonna behave herself.

"Go find your mother and not a word or the doll gets it." Not like she wasn't gonna tear the shit apart anyway. I watched her leave the room in a huff, taking her sweet time, but now I had another problem on my hand and I could see on the faces of the others that they had just come to the same conclusion.

"You mind telling me how you knew she was in here?" The connecting door slid open and he was just there. "How the fuck did you get in my house?" The fucker smirked at me.

"Gentlemen, if you want my help we've got work to do." We all looked at each other but what the fuck could we say? "I still wanna know how you got in here." I know my security is good, and my men are all over this place like flies on shit, so if this fuck had just walked by them and bypassed my safety then he wasn't just good, he was fucking Teflon.

"How I got here is of no consequence and yes Lyon I know for a man like you that's hard to swallow, but it's just gonna have to do for now. Now, Khalil, the Porters, the fuck up." He looked at Law when he said that and I'm sure we were all remembering that first conference call.

"Are you a spook?" I hate those fucks like poison and from the look of disgust on his face so did he. "Since we don't know each other I'd try not to see that as an insult. What I am is not important for now, but you can Google me, I'm a restaurateur."

"My ass." Logan wasn't looking too pleased. I guess he didn't like anyone being more of a spook than him. Mancini just smiled and pulled up a seat like he owned the place. One thing was clear; this was no biker type. He's exactly what I would've been if Elena had got her hooks in me as a teen.

He was well dressed, well groomed and I guess what the women would call fuck hot. There wasn't a hair out of place and butter wouldn't melt in his mouth. But it was in the eyes; they were the eyes of a killer.

"I have to be gone in about an hour so if there're any questions let's get them out of the way."
"Why? You'll just tell us they're of no consequence."
"Justice, how are you?"

"I'm cool, nice to finally meet the man behind the name, now you wanna tell us what the fuck we're dealing with here?"

He studied each of us like we were under a microscope and as much as I admired his style I was getting tired of his shit. "Bro put up or get to wherever the fuck you need to be early. I don't have time for games and I sure as fuck don't have any to waste. I get it, you're good at whatever the fuck it is you do, but so am I, and every man in this room. Your name came from someone I trust, that's the only reason I haven't capped your ass for sneaking into my house."

He grinned and looked at my watch. "Your little toy there told you the minute I breached. I wasn't expecting a civilian to have such technology, that one slipped right by me." The others looked at me but I didn't have to explain myself. I go all out to protect what's mine and if that means buying shit off the black market so be it.

"That ought to teach you to go playing around in other people's backyards." I whistled and Jared and Tommy came out of their hiding places. "We're cool go keep an eye on the women we'll be out soon."

Now I had the others eyeing my ass, like I was gonna share all my secrets. It wasn't that I didn't trust them, but there are no lengths I wouldn't go to-to keep my family safe. I'm sure these boys were of the same mind.

"So what do you have for us Mancini? Our women aren't the most patient bunch." Connor was cool as a cucumber as he held up the wall.
"What I have is a conspiracy. These players are into more shit than a little bit. We have trafficking, sex slaves, pedophilic rings, murder and espionage. What you boys walked into goes way beyond what's going on-on the waterfront in that little town of yours."

"How much did you know about your commander?" He turned his attention to the SEALs who all stepped towards him like they were ready to tear him apart. "He was clean, I don't give a fuck what you think you know that much we do know. So if you're here to sell us anything different you can get fucked."

"Take it easy Tyler, I'm inclined to agree with you. I asked because he had more than you've found. He was killed…"

"You know this for a fact?" It was Logan's turn to move on him. I was lost. I hadn't heard shit about the fucks that had put my daughter in that book, other than the mention of their name.

"Yes."
"Who?"
"I'm not at liberty..."
"You say that shit one more time..."
"Cool it, everyone to their corners. Look Mancini show us your cards or get out of the game." That's what I get for playing along with these organized fucks. I could've been to the desert and back ten times by now and put an end to this shit. The fuck I give a fuck about espionage?

"Gentlemen, I understand your frustration, and believe me I'm not interested in protecting these fuckers any more than you are. But there are things involved that if not handled carefully can backfire on us, and yes that us meant I am throwing my hat in the ring. Like I said I have somewhere to be, I just dropped in to take your measure so to speak, see who it was I am getting into bed with. I'll be in touch."

The fucker got up and left the way he came. "Uh, am I the only one who's confused?"

"No Law, I think we're all in the dark on this one." Smooth motherfucker, he might've pissed me off coming into my place the way he did, but I had to give him his due.

"That's Mancini, I'm surprised he even showed up here." Creed looked after the door where he'd disappeared.

"This other guy Thorpe, what the fuck is he like?"

"I don't think he's as hard core as that one, Law but he's no light weight either."

What the fuck did I get myself into? The guy is good, the way he came in, had I not had my place rigged he would've blown past my security. My guys hadn't seen him, but I was warned just before the phone rang and that's what tipped me off.

"So what just happened here?" Quinn, one of the least heard from SEALs spoke up. "He just appeared, said some shit that we already knew and left, what was the purpose?"

"Just what he said, taking our measure; I get the feeling he knows more about us than we do him." I wasn't sure how to feel about that shit.

"I think he did a little bit more than that, I think he just warned us about what we're really dealing with here. What was that crack about the commander? He said it almost as if he knows something. He said 'he knew more than what we've found."

"What I wanna know is how the fuck he knows what we found Cord. Until Lyon mentioned this guy I never heard of him. We've looked since he came up and all we found was the billionaire bullshit. That's no mere billionaire that just left this room."

"You're right Dev, this guy whatever, whoever he is, he's under deep, but I still say he was giving us a hint. And he knows who killed the CO I want that information. Then I want to go after the fuckers one at a time and skin the flesh from their bodies."

"You and me both brother, looks like we have shit to do, fuck." Logan paced the room deep in thought. I could only imagine what these boys were feeling. I'd heard some of what had been going on with them, had heard about the old man who'd taken them all under his wing. I couldn't imagine anyone fucking with Daniel so I felt their pain.

"We need to get this shit together boys, there're too many things going on at once. We can't do this now with a house full of people, but we need to get this shit sorted and soon. Everyone seems to agree on one point, this desert fuck isn't coming here because of the trafficking we need to find out why he's coming. Seems to me that's the most important thing at this point. We find that we may be able to get in front of this thing."

"Lyon's right, in the meantime, Susie was in that book and I need to know why. She wasn't mine when that picture was taken so how did Khalil know and why her? I think we know." He looked at his brothers as he spoke. "We need the targets, let's go through that book again and take another look at the girls in there, maybe something in there will lead us to something."

"Wait, what did I miss? You know why she was in there?"
"We think we do but it's not something we can discuss until we've spoken to the parties involved, believe me it's nothing that will hurt this."

"The fuck, you spook types take lessons from each other? I find it strange that I'm about the only one who doesn't have shit to hide. I know why my kid was in there, the Porters. Law, your girl was in there why?"

"The fucker that paid her father off killed my family or had them killed, I don't know why she was in the book, other than that he wanted a Stepford wife or some fuck."

"And you Creed?"
"Her fucked up aunt sold her out."
I studied the room, there was something there but what the fuck that was I couldn't put my finger on it. I watched each man in turn, the way they stood, almost at attention. The way their eyes were directed one way but I could tell they were very aware of everything that was going on in the room.

"I think I've got it. You boys were all in some branch of the military at some point weren't you? Any chance all of you worked for this commander at some point?" The room came alive then, everyone started talking at once.

"I'm guessing that's right?" They all nodded but there was nothing else forthcoming, I guess that was top-secret shit too. "Fine, so maybe whatever this fuck is after has something to do with the commander. What did spook boy say, he knew more than you've found? Where have you been looking?"

"Well fuck, we've got to head back." "Not today Lo. We promised these girls a good holiday away from the bullshit and this is baby Zak's first Xmas and that fuck don't get to mess with that fuck no."
"Ty what is it with you and that kid?"
"What do you mean?" He looked at me like I was the crazy one.
"Nothing, nothing at all." Well he was gone.

"Right, let's go salvage what we can of the rest of the day before these women revolt." We'd only been gone an hour or so but it felt much longer. We each got glares and rolled eyes from our women but no one said anything.

"Good afternoon Mr. Lyon I'd like you to meet my parents." Fucker ambushed me as soon as I came out the room. It was on the tip of my tongue to rip into his dad for not keeping his ass home and away from my kid, but the rational part of my brain, the

part that Kat and her kids hadn't fucked up,
knew that was an asshole way to think.

So I outstretched my hand and played
nice. Turns out, the dad is some hotshot
engineer and the mom's a medical
researcher. They seemed cool enough and
the mother Doreen seemed fond of my kid.
"So, I hear you're moving soon." The kid
walked away after making the introductions.
Probably off to go sniffing around my
daughter.

"Tomorrow to be exact, Todd wanted
to spend one last Xmas with our girl before
he left and we couldn't deny him." What the
fuck?
"Our girl?"
"Oh yes, Caitlin, we're very fond of her,
very bright, sweet, disciplined. Just the kind
of girl we would've chosen for Todd had he
not had the foresight to find her himself."

Did this fuck even know how close he
was to taking a header out the nearest
fucking window? "You talking about my
fifteen year old daughter?" He didn't exactly
smirk but there was some kind of look on
his face that wasn't gonna last long.

"Don't misunderstand Colton, I may
call you Colton correct? Look we

understand your position, if Todd was any other kid we would be having the same issue, but our son is a very well rounded kid with a good head on his shoulder. We've already spoken to him about the dangers of going too far at their age, things like that."

"You talked about my daughter having sex?" this fuck was two steps away from a pine box. What the fuck was it about this holiday and people fucking with me? "Not exactly, but I did have a talk with my son about his responsibility to your daughter. Look, Todd knows you don't approve of him, all I'm saying is that I get it, but you don't have anything to worry about."

I studied him. His words sounded like textbook bullshit to me, but the man had every right to talk to his son. The fact that he was full of shit was another matter. "Look, you can spout all the crap you want, but we both know kids are gonna do whatever the fuck they want in the end. You're right, I'm not happy with the relationship, but my kid thinks she's in love. The fact that you're moving might've saved your kid. I don't dislike Todd, but I don't want my daughter that deeply involved with anyone until she's thirty."

"You have to know that's not realistic." He smiled while his wife started to look nervous. "What I know is that it's good your kid is leaving, no disrespect but you seem to be all gung-ho about this shit, I'm not. And she's nobody's girl but mine." I walked away from them just a little more pissed than I'd already been.

At least that shit had taken my mind off the fuckery in the study for a hot minute. I went in search of my kids it was their day after all. They were knee deep in new shit and making enough noise to raise the roof, but they were happy.

Nothing that was going on had or will ever touch them. "This is what it's all about, them, keeping them safe." Law came up beside me in the doorway where I was peeping in on them. "That's what I'm most worried about, how the fuck do we keep them safe when we're all spread out all over the place?'

The others came to join us. "We were just discussing that. The way this thing is panning out, we're gonna have to watch each other's six, we have to weed out the bad seeds starting now because we all know money trumps most anything when it comes to the lesser known."

"My guys are safe, I don't surround myself with fucks. They've all been with me for many years and those who weren't aren't close enough to get at me and mine." He had a point though, if what Mancini said was on point and I had no reason to doubt him, then these fuckers were gonna be gunning for us.

I didn't kid myself that if they were as cold as he intimated that they didn't already know everyone that was involved here. "Anyone got the sense that they were under the scope? I didn't think about it before today, the fact that they might know we're onto them. That Stockton fuck is dead but who knows who was watching him."

"We're way ahead of you, the compound is secure and there's more than enough room for everyone if it comes to that."
"Thanks Lo but I'm not running from these fucks, I have shit to do, they're kids out there depending on me to come stand guard at the drop of a hat. I can't just drop everything and go into hiding like a pussy because of these bureaucratic assholes."

"Creed, think about Jess."
"I wish those motherfuckers would. They had their one chance already, any fuck even

looks at her too long I'm dropping 'em." I could get behind that.

"Gentlemen."

"What the fuck?" Mallory snuck up behind us.

"I understand you met the great Mancini; Lyon I gave Kat the loot for the kids."

"Brother, where're yours, where's Lydia?"

"She's in there with her nosy ass, the kids are with mom and pop, I didn't want to expose the other kids to whatever the fuck some fuck sent his kid to school with that made my boy sick. I find out who this asshole is I'ma go rip the fuck apart."

"The kid?"

"Nah the father. Who the fuck sends his kid to school with a hundred other kids knowing he's contagious?" Crazy fucks, I'm surrounded.

"Anyway what did you boys think of Mancini?" He smirked and shoved his hands in his pockets.

"Where the fuck did you find him? Spook's R'Us?" Tyler, fucker thinks too much like me, it's eerie.

"Nah, he's my cousin and that's all I'm prepared to say. By the way did anyone think to warn Summers and Masters to watch their backs until we can get with them?"

"I did, I've been keeping them up to date, but now with what your cousin told us today I'm not sure that's enough. I'll feel like shit if anything happens to those boys, I'm the one who brought them in."
"No worries Law, I had a look at those boys and they can hold their own. By the way boys my old man said to tell you anything you need. He hates these fucks almost as much as we do."

"Why, what did they do to him?" This ought to be good.
"Other than fucking with Caitlin? He heard politician and went off on one of his tangents."
"What's he got against politicians?"
"Says they're all shylocks, thieves and liars." This from a man who's spent more than half his life on the FBI's most wanted list.

We walked away from the door and headed back to the women. Kat's gonna light into my ass later if I keep this shit up on her big day. Her eyes gravitated to me as soon as I entered the room. My sweet girl was still looking a bit sullen around the mouth, and her eyes didn't have that light that I love so much.

"You did a great job here baby thanks." I pulled her up from the chair where she'd been sitting having a talk with Creed's woman. The men were finding their women and from the looks of things there was a lot of making up going around.

"You having a good day baby?" She nodded with a small smile and I smelt her hair as I folded her into me. It felt like forever since I'd touched her, it was always this way after one of our little skirmishes. Now the need to reseal the bond was strong and I had a houseful of damn people. Not that that would stop me, but there was too many variables in my place for me to fuck around.

"You met Todd's parents I see. What pray tell did you tell them to have them speaking in hushed tones and giving you wary looks?"
"I told them if their son came near my kid I'd chuck his ass out the nearest window."

"Colton." She hissed and pulled her head back with her usual glare. I looked down at her still after all this time trying to see what it was about her that totally did it for me. I sometimes wondered if the people around us had that kind of love, if each man in this room felt that all consuming emotion that wraps around your heart and squeeze?

"What are you looking at Colton?"
"The most amazing thing in the world." Her eyes grew wet and softer as I kissed her brow. "Did you go snooping upstairs babe?" She shook her head but I know she's a lying ass. Mad or not, I know she'd go searching for the one special gift I get her every year. She's worse than the kids with that shit, tearing my place apart. This time I'd outfoxed her though, her and her nosy ass kids whom she always enlists for help.

"What did you get me?"
"Maybe I won't give it to you, bad girls don't deserve presents."
"Hmm, I wonder what should be the punishment for bad boys?"
"I'm never bad baby, how're your legs, need me to put some salve on them?" This is why she always gets away with shit. I spank her ass, she pouts, I feel guilty and cave.

"Maybe later, the day has barely just started and I have all these people to look after and it's almost time to eat."

"What the fuck they been doing the last four
hours?"
"Picking Colton, hors d'oeuvres and finger
foods. We have a nice spread prepared
you'll love it."

The day turned out way better than it
begun, the guys and I were able to put it
aside for the rest of the day and enjoy our
families. I looked around the table that
looked so different from the year before. All
these new faces, brought together by tragedy
but quickly becoming one of us.

I liked the way they treated their
women, saw the same heart that beat in my
chest in them in the way they were so
fucking gone, the lengths they were willing
to go to-to protect. I knew that in the coming
days things were gonna be rough, knew that
there was no getting out from under this shit
we were facing without casualties, but there
was no way I was gonna lose any one of
them.

They were now my brothers, a bond
forged in fire, I'd do for them what I would
for Jared or Tommy, or any one of my boys.
Now with the holiday coming to a close, it
was time to get to work doing what I do
best, look out for me and mine.

Chapter 17
Todd
***

"Todd, what're you doing? My dad would kill us if he caught us out here alone?" She looked around as if expecting him to appear out of the darkness. She's so pretty under the moonlight it hurts. The feelings I have inside for her scare me, I don't know if I can make it without her. I've been fighting with my parents to find a way for me to stay, had explained to them that even the thought of leaving her makes me feel like my life was ending.

They were more understanding than I thought they would be. My dad is always so caught up in his work I never thought he had any time to notice what was going on around him, and mom, well she's mom. She thinks every little thing will hurt me, just like when I was five.

We'd had a long talk the three of us about my relationship with Caitlin, my Caitlin. If only her dad was half as understanding then I wouldn't have this knot in my gut. If anyone else comes near her while I'm gone I'll end them. But for now I have to make sure she's okay, she's been having as hard a time with this as I have.

"Caitie, I know what your dad thinks, I know what a lot of people think, but I'm never gonna make you do anything you don't wanna. You see this." I lifted my shirt and showed her the surprise I had waiting, one of her Xmas gifts, her name tattooed across my heart.

"Todd, oh my gosh did it hurt?" She ran her finger gently over the letters, under the concern I sensed the pride. "No it didn't hurt, whatever I felt it was worth it, to have you with me all the time. This means that I'll wait for you no matter what. You're too young we're both too young I know that. For now, I just wanna spend as much time with you as I can just to look at your face. Because seeing your face is like every Xmas and birthday I've ever had rolled into one. And one day, when the time is right we'll have our forever. Don't cry, you know I hate it when you cry come 'ere."

I pulled her into my chest just as I saw the shadow disappear behind the door leading outside. One guess as to who that was, but I was still breathing so maybe he'd heard enough to know. That didn't stop my guts from tightening in fear though. Mr. Lyon is one scary guy. I wonder how he'd feel if he knew I wanted to be just like him when I grow up.

Epilogue 1
Lyon
***

It's been almost a month since Xmas and I still hadn't gone to the desert. I gave my word that I would let those boys work their shit, but each day was getting harder and harder. Mancini had been in touch since that first meet and from his smarmy comments I gathered he was working behind the scenes but the fucker was still keeping us in the dark. No one had made a move on my family thus far so I was giving these military fuck types the benefit of the doubt. How long that would last was up for grabs.

"Hi honey guess what?" She was pretty chipper when I got home that evening as she flitted around the kitchen finishing up dinner. I eyed her ass because the only time she gets like this is when she and her posse get up to some shit that I'm not gonna like.

"What did you and my pain in the ass mother do now?"

"Nothing, Todd's back isn't that great? His parents are here to tie up some loose ends for the weekend. I almost said thank heavens the fuck was back until I saw what was sitting in my living room what the fuck? Where did they take him a farm where they overfeed kids or some fuck. "Who the fuck is that?"

"That's Todd doesn't he look great? Caitie is so excited." She was smiling and clapping her hands and shit like this was a good thing.

"That is no kid in there that's a grown fucking man. The fucking kid looks too grown, I don't want him around my daughter." I think I'm gonna have a heart attack.

"Colton you're being unreasonable now, you need to calm down and think rationally. Do you really want to hurt Caitlin? He's only home for a few days let them have their time."

Why is she always fucking with me? "Where the fuck is the pothead with the pipe? You see that, are you happy now? Look what you've turned me into, you and your damn kids."

"Oh so now they're mine?"

"Daddy, you're shouting again, that can't be good for…" The little one came out of nowhere with her shit.

"Mengele take your ass in the basement and blow some shit up." Fuck, the little shit's eyes lit up as she turned to head that way. "Come back here you." Fucking criminal in the making. I gave her mother the stink eye because this was all her damn fault. Daughters and shit, I warned her this fuckery was gonna happen.

***

Epilogue 2
Lyon
***

"I don't know what the fuck's wrong with her, but she's gonna tell me tonight or somebody's getting an ass whipping." I don't know if it's the stuff I'm dealing with, the fact that I haven't been able to share it with her, but some fuck was going on.

"Colt, you know you can't handle everything with anger right?"

"The fuck are you on? I just told you Kat's been moping around the house for the past two days, even the kids can't get a rise outta her and you tell me fuck all? How else am I supposed to get her ass back on track?"

My wife and kids are on a mission to make me fucking crazy. The boys aren't so bad; it's the fucking females in my house that are all about to get a boot in the ass starting with their mother. My Caitie Bear has some kid sitting on my couch every evening like he lives there or some fuck and the little one is trying her best to land in the pen before she reach ten with her criminal mind ass, and now this fuckery.

"You ever stop to think she might be depressed?" I looked at him like he was out his fucking mind.
"What the fuck? What does she have to be depressed about? The only thing I don't do for my wife is breathe you fuck, and as much time as I spend watching her sleep I might as well be doing that shit too."

Jared held up his hands and grinned at me. "You think you're ever gonna be rational where she's concerned? It's been what, fifteen, sixteen years, and you're still hotheaded as fuck when it comes to her."

"I don't see what the fuck that has to do with her moping shit." He rolled his eyes at me, the fuck.

"It doesn't, it has to do with you thinking you can fight all her battles for her." I'm about to knock him the fuck out friend or no friend. "Who the fuck is supposed to do it? And why the fuck do you think my wife is depressed?"

"Colton, do you not remember the reason she moved here in the first place?" What the fuck? "Yeah, she came here to find me." The rest of that business does not bare thinking about. "Fuck."

"Where're you going?"
"Home to my wife you dumb fuck where do you think?" I did not appreciate his laughter; I'll deal with his shit tomorrow. Fucking depression and shit, if that's what's bothering her I'll go into the fucking desert and find the coyotes that ate that fuck and kill his ass again, the fuck.

"Elena, you at my house?" Like she'd be anywhere else in the middle of the damn afternoon with her nosy ass.
"Hello son, nice to hear you too."
"Listen old lady, don't give me any shit I need a favor."

"What son? Anything."

"I need you to take the kids and bounce." The little fucks were home for some asshole's birthday or some fuck. No wonder my wife was losing her damn mind, fucking Catalina alone would send a priest to the fucking psych ward with her shit.

"Catalina too?" See what I mean?"
Still.
"You got a problem with my kid?"
"Uh no but do you know what she gets up to with your father?"
"As long as he's not sharing the pipe I don't give a fu…"
"Colton Lyon you watch your mouth."

"Ma…kids…out…now."
"Oh alright, but I think something's wrong with Kat." Her voice had gone soft there at the end.
"Yeah I know, I'm gonna take care of it."
Fuck if I can't.

****

The house was clear when I got there; even the baby was gone. Shit gave me a start for a second. It's been a while since Hitler's youth or one of the others hasn't been here to greet me. "Kat?" I walked through the house getting pissed by the second.

She was in bed with the covers up to her chin. I took a deep breath and tried for calm. Instead of yelling the house down like I wanted to, I just kicked off my shit kickers and crawled into bed behind her. "Colton you're home."

"Yeah baby I'm home." Her voice sounded so little and lost, and then a thought hit me that had my guts going cold. "Swear to fuck Kat if you're sick I'm gonna be pissed way the fuck off, look at me." She started to giggle snort. That's a start at least, even though I was sure she was laughing at me.

"What kinda sense does that make crazy person?"
"You're not sick?" My hand went to her heart where I could feel it beating strong and full of life. She shook her head no. "Then what is it?"
She sat up in bed and bent her knees. With her chin resting on them she turned to look at me.

"I think I need to go…"
"You're not going any fucking where I'll kill your ass first, what the fuck is this shit Katarina." I jumped off the bed like the shit

was on fire. It was either that or strangle her
ass.
"Colton will you calm down?"

"Don't tell me to calm down when
you're about to send my ass to jail for
twenty to life, cause swear to fuck I'd break
your fucking neck. Then what would happen
to our kids, or were you even thinking about
them? And if you think you're taking my
fucking kids anywhere you're out your
fucking mind, no one is leaving this fucking
house."

She was just staring at me like I'd lost
my shit. "Colton, are you nuts, what the hell
goes through your head for heavens sake?"
She face palmed and shook her head.
"That's not what you were getting at?"

"No caveman Dan, I was going to say
I think I need to go to a different doctor."
"Why, what's wrong with your present
quack?" My heart was doing fucking
cartwheels in my chest.
She reached into the nightstand and got out
an envelope.

I was expecting some kind of medical
report but instead I was looking at a
sonogram. The shit looked like mass
confusion to me. "The fuck am I looking at

Kat?" Fuck if I know. She got to her knees and leaned into me.

"You see here, and here, and here, and..." She kept going with that shit and I still didn't know what she was telling me. "English for the idiot husband that you are so fond of calling me when you think I'm not within earshot." I smirked at her because she'd got her ass beat more than once for that shit.

"It's babies Colt." Ookay, we have like ten of the little fucks already, I'd lost count. Her words registered and my head started to spin. She was pregnant. But why was she so sad? She's never been like this with any of the others.

"You mad because Cody's still so little?"
"Colton there are three babies in there and note the absence of anything down south?" The fuck was she going on about now? We had twins already what was one more?

"I don't follow, what, you're depressed because you don't want to have anymore kids? You do know that fucking without protection usually leads to that shit right?" Now I was really getting pissed, then her words registered.

"Fuck no Kat you promised." We were both holding onto each other for support now. "I don't think it's up to me, but this can't be right can it? I mean we just had the baby and oh crap Colt, three girls, at once, like Catalina."

"Okay-okay let's not panic, your quack has been known to be wrong before." I had to walk this shit off. I think my dick had crawled into my ass. Good for him greedy fuck, this was all his fault.

"We can't give them to Elena and the pothead, too old, your parents, same fuckery. Maybe we're jumping the gun here, maybe they won't…fuck me Kat no more girls that was the deal. Oh fuck don't do that." I went to her side and took her into my arms. She was starting that crying shit that always makes me stupid.

I rolled my eyes over her head when she blubbered into my chest. I should kick Jared's ass, dumb fuck. Depressed my ass, she was hormonal. Oh joy. "Kat, baby, exactly what is it that you're afraid of?" I knew she wasn't really afraid of another Mengele, she loves that damn kid, thinks she's the female version of me.

"I was just getting rid of my paunch Colton." I wasn't even gonna entertain that shit. There was only one way to prove shit to her. She always gets weepy and emotional when she's breeding, that shit made me snort out loud. "What's so funny?"

She wiped her damn nose in my shirt. "That's some nasty shit. I think I know when I nailed you. It's when you and your posse were being sneaky with Caitie Bear and the fucking dead teen walking."

Now she was the one rolling her eyes and trying to escape me. "Uh-uh-uh lemme see." My dick was already getting hard with anticipation. If I told her now with her hormones going crazy just how much I love fucking my kids into her she'd pitch a fit. My hand was already heading for her ass, which was always the first thing to spread.

"Quit it Colt, that's how we got into this mess in the first place."
"Deed's already done." I was already busy getting her naked. "Oh yeah, you're well and truly bred Katarina." I rubbed my dick in her ass and took her down while she laughed and tried to throw me off. At least she wasn't sulking anymore.

A pregnant Kat is like a magnet for my dick. I made quick work and had her robe off in no time, and was soon stepping out of my pants. Just the thought that my kids were in her womb was enough to get me off so I had to throttle back, didn't want her laughing at my ass.

"Stay right there baby-just like that." I stroked my cock while she looked over her shoulder at me all coy and shit. She was in the middle of our bed on her hands and knees, her already full tits hanging low and her ass in the air. "I want that ass higher, don't make me have to go digging for the pussy." She canted her ass the way I like and I moved in behind her.

I spread her pussy open from behind and stuck my tongue down inside her. I licked her walls making her twitch in my hands that were holding her fast. She moved against my mouth taking my tongue deeper. "Hurry Colton." I guess I didn't move fast enough because my greedy girl pulled off my tongue, twisted her body around, and swallowed my dick whole.

I smacked her ass so she'd feed me her pussy again, and we ended up in a sixty-nine. I'd added one more piercing over the years because she loves that shit, makes her pussy yowl. She had some fun playing with them with her tongue and making my ass crazy.

"I wanna cum inside you ease off." She lifted her head off my dick and made her way down my body. She sat on my cock reverse cowgirl and did her thing. "Fuck yeah, shit." I grabbed fistfuls of her ass as she fucked herself hard on my cock. "Shh, baby, come 'ere." She was trying to outrun the shit in her head.

I sat up behind her and wrapped my arms around her. "We're always going to be fine Kat no matter what. You have to carry them but you know I'm going to be here for you every step of the way. You're beautiful, and you're going to be even more so when the babies grow inside you." I was trying to head off the fuckery she'd dealt with-with this last pregnancy.

For some fucked up reason women seemed to think that their bodies were supposed to stop doing what they were made for just because they were getting older. I'm sure some fucked up asshole put that out there. I'd like to meet the fuck and gut him. How was I supposed to convince her that this was her most beautiful period when some expert asshole was always telling women how to lose baby weight two seconds after giving birth? Backwards fuck.

I soon had her on her hands and knees again driving into her from behind. I hit her pussy end on each stroke until she was grabbing the sheets and fucking back at me the way I like. I was on a mission to erase every doubt and fear from her mind. I ran my fingers over the piercing in her pussy, while trailing the ink of my name in her back with the fingers of the other.

Her body shook and she came while my cock kept growing inside her. It never failed, for the next week or so her pregnancy was going to make me randy as fuck. That means I'm going to be in her every time she blinks, talk about hair of the dog.

I let my hands do the talking and when that wasn't enough I turned her around to face me. "I want to see you, I want to see my babies when I cum inside you." I slid out of her, laid her down beneath me and slid back into her wet heat. "I love the fuck outta fucking you baby." I moved inside her letting her feel the strength and length of my cock.

I moved back so that I wasn't crushing her into the mattress and looked down between us at the little paunch that never quite went away after the last baby came. My dick got hard as fuck at the sight of it, my seed was in there, growing, three of them, fuck. "How was ever I so fucking lucky to deserve you baby?" She lifted her mouth to meet mine and I was sure that the tears in her eyes were ones of joy.

THE END

EXCLUSIVE LOOK AT MARKED #3
(Marked Series)
Pre-Order Link:

http://amzn.com/B018OUHZ5K

2

"They were just leaving."

Miranda eyed them with annoyance clear on her face. "I believe I told you that she wouldn't be ready to speak with you until after she was given the all clear. What part of 'head trauma' and 'is under strict order to not be upset in any way,' did you not understand?"

Gulver stepped forward, palms up, while he spoke to her. "It's important that we speak to the victim of the crime as soon as they are conscious. So much information is still fresh—"

"Knock it off, Officer. You and I both know the procedure…not my first merry-go-round. If the doctor or I say that you need to wait, you wait until the patient is physically and mentally prepared to do so. Their well-being should be top priority."

"We understand, but she has—"

"She," Maya sneered at them, hand clutching mine in a tight grip, "is right here, and would appreciate it if you would stop speaking about her as if she has no say in the matter." The machine beside her beeped, and all eyes inside the room shifted. Her blood pressure was rising and rapidly.

Fuck this. "We will speak to you after I get her cleaned up and she has eaten, and not a second sooner. Janice and Brian won't disappear while she takes care of her needs."

"So you know who attacked her? How?" Again, Gulver with his shit. He's more than lucky to have that badge protecting him.

"For fuck's sake," Maya growled out in warning, pushing against the hand I had on her shoulder keeping her in place. "I told him the second I woke up…now get out!"

"Ms. Owens—" This time Marquez stepped forward. Done. They'd pushed my girl too far and I was ready to deck the motherfucker, consequences be damned. His eyes met mine and widened, my ire growing with each second that passed.

Before I could move or say another word, Maya's nurse stepped in. "Leave, or I will report you for harassing my patient and her fiancé."

"We're just trying to do our jobs."

"I'm sorry," Marquez interjected, voice contrite. "We never meant for this to escalate or upset Ms. Owens. Talan," he called out, and I nodded, "please call me when she's ready. Let's go." With that, he turned and pulled a now quiet Gulver toward the door. Without another word the two exited the room, leaving us alone with her nurse.

"Assholes couldn't wait a few hours," Miranda mumbled and I laughed, breaking a bit of the tension inside the hospital room. Craziness followed me everywhere.

"Agreed." Turning toward my girl, I leaned down until we were at eye level. This was the perfect example of a moment where my anger had to be tamed and her needs put first. "Can you try and calm down for me? Breathe in and out. I'm here, and I'm not leaving." Bitty gifted me one of her pretty smiles. "Good girl." And then I got an eye roll and a weak slap on the arm.

"Honey, you are screwed," came

from Miranda over by the two monitors next to the bed, watching as the numbers of Maya's blood pressure began to drop. My own anxiousness seemed to evaporate as Maya calmed down.

"Who's 'honey'?" I had to ask. Curiosity was a bitch.

"Applies to both," she snickered and continued to write her reading on Maya's chart. Women.

"Hey, Miranda?" Maya called out after a few minutes of silence, gaining her attention. "Can you unplug me from the machines? I want to get cleaned up."

"Maya, I told you—"

"I won't let anything happen to her." At my interjection she huffed, but after a few speculative minutes, she nodded.

"Get me fired, and you'll be maintaining me for the rest of my life."

I waved her on. "Duly noted."

"You two are adorable yet sickeningly sweet. How's that even possible?"

"Thank you, Miranda…now unplug me, woman." Bitty ignored her, choosing instead to focus her attention toward the matter at hand.

"You heard the patient." Had to add my two cents.

"Impatient little… You both better behave."

After her nurse left with a few admonishments about proper hospital etiquette, I pecked my girl's lips and stood up. Looking down at her, I was once again hit with just how tiny my Bitty was. Sure, she was curvy. Had an amazing ass and the perfect-sized tits, but in stature, she was small. Petite. Delicate.

The bruising over her temple stood out against her tan skin. Dark and angry. Everything my girl wasn't. To think that someone would hurt her… Fuck! I needed to stop that train of thought before the anger I fought with daily consumed me.

She needed me.

More than ever, Bitty needed me.

"Give me five minutes to set things up," I informed her, the tips of my fingers running down her cheek until I cupped her jaw. "Don't move."

At my admonishment, Maya rolled her eyes while holding her pinky up to me. "Promise." And then, she pushed herself off the bed to reach me. There was that look in her eye, the one that told me just how much pain she was in. Fucking gutted me. Because to her, I was worth it.

My kisses.

My touch.

Our love.

I met her halfway and pressed my lips to hers. Urgent. Desperation so intense hit me from all angles. She moaned as my fingers wove themselves into her hair and massaged her scalp, soft touches to help soothe her.

Maya arched into me, the movement sudden and hurtful. "Fuck," she whimpered out, and I froze.

"Don't move." Her hands, which had

been in my hair, tugged hard, keeping me from pulling away as I should have. Insane, defenseless when it came to her, I nodded against her lips and kissed her slowly. This girl drove me insane, but I understood. We fed off each other. Yearned for the closeness.

I would never—and could never—deny her.

"Look at me, baby." Gorgeous grey eyes opened and met my own. In them I saw her love for me, and my heart raced. "I love you." Lips parted, and her breath became my own. Fed my lungs what was vital for me to live. "Have since the day you walked into my shop all sass and bark. Fucking bowled me over with your beauty, but it was your heart that stole mine. Please don't ever return it; it's yours. Just like you will always fucking be mine."

Because that was what I did; I lived for—and because of—her.

"You own me, Talan. No one will ever take me away."

One more peck on the lips, and then

I pushed off the bed, walked over to Maya's bag on the floor, and picked it up.

Bitty was very particular about which products she used. She'd hate anything the hospital would provide, so like a good boyfriend, and because I refused to leave her side, I had Esther buy her everything she would need.

Not that she complained. This had meant free access to my credit card and shopping for her best friend. My only request was that she did it quickly, and that she treated herself to something for all the help. Esther had readily agreed, and my Bitty had been thrilled to have things that reminded her of home.

Our home. The one we would share until we were old and grey. Cranky fuckers fighting over the remote control and which show we'd watch. The same home where she would slap my hand each time I copped a feel of her ass.

"Growing old will be fun with this

chick," I muttered once inside the bathroom because I was no fool. Maya remembered everything and made me pay for it later.

Turning the shower on, I adjusted the temperature knob and let the hot water warm the room.

Shampoo and conditioners—yes, more than one bottle—were placed inside the small shower niche, a tiny alcove that barely contained the three bottles. Next, I placed her Victoria's Secret lotion and body mist on the shelf above the toilet, hair brush and comb next to them, and then her toothbrush, toothpaste, and deodorant. Face wash and other crap that I didn't understand stayed inside the small carry-on Esther bought.

Christ, do women need a lot of shit.

Shaking my head, I walked out and gingerly picked her up and off the bed. "Come on, pretty girl, let's get you cleaned up."

"Thank God." Maya sighed and leaned her head on my chest, nuzzling and taking in a deep inhale of my scent. I kissed the top of her head before placing her on her feet. Too cute.

"Let's get you naked." Giggles rang out of the small room as I lecherously waggled my eyebrows while removing her hospital gown. Warmed my fucking heart to hear her so carefree. Then, that laughter died—gone, just as fast as it had arrived.

"Bitty, what…" The small mirror above the sink. Motherfuck. "Baby, it's just bruising. It'll all go away in time." No reaction. Instead, her eyes stood transfixed on the small piece-of-shit object that hung on the wall. Linda and Mathew had been dead set on not letting her see the bruising that had developed on over half her face. It was the wrong call. Told them as much.

Fuck.

Watery eyes stared back at her reflection. "Oh my God." Three words. The pitch in her tone was even and resolute, as if she had no more fight left in her.

Cupping her jaw, I turned her sad face toward my own. "Stop it."

"Talan, look at what she—"

"You are beautiful." Her beauty was more than just superficial; my Bitty had a heart of gold.

A long sigh escaped her, and she looked down. "It's not the bruising that hurts me, Talan. It's seeing what she did—reliving it all over again."

"Fuck her."

"How can I forget? Dammit, look at me!"

"When did I ever tell you to forget?"

"It was implied." An annoyed huff which ended with her hand on her hip followed. *Stubborn fucking woman. How could she even think that?*

"I'd never be so insensitive as to say that. Maya, I said fuck her…everything she stands for, not what she did and will pay for with blood."

Her face softened at that, and the hand on her hip fell beside her. "You promised me."

"Let's get you cleaned up before the

water turns cold." Maya pursed her lips but didn't argue. With a soft touch, I pulled her lace panties down and threw them inside the small waste container in the room. Those wouldn't be needed.

Nothing she wore inside this place would be coming home with us.

3

"God, I needed this." Her moan…fuck. Low and sultry, the sound of her pleasure made me hard as fuck. Like granite, smooth and slick against her heated flesh, rubbing itself into her lower back and leaving a trail of pre-come while my hands focused on lathering her front.

I'd tossed the washcloth Esther had bought for her in the trash the moment we'd stepped inside the small shower. Wasn't needed. My hands were more than enough to take care of her needs.

"I needed you." Truth. My truth. Maya was the only thing that mattered to me, and the fear that had gripped me that night—seeing her unconscious—nearly killed me. Drove me past what was considered sane by society. Blood and revenge was all I had wanted, and still do, but now I have to be thankful and enjoy our connection.

A shift, a small swivel of her hips, and her ass ground against me. "Need you now."

"Son of a bitch, Maya." A resounding thwack reverberated inside the bathroom as my palm connected with the all-white tiled wall. "Behave." It was meant as a warning, one she didn't adhere to. No, instead she pushed back again. Harder this time. Too much and not enough. She was a goddamned vision standing there beneath the water. Wet. Rivulets of water cascading down her body, tempting me.

Without preamble, no warning, I cupped her hot little pussy in my hand and added the tiniest bit of pressure.

"Please, baby. Just help me forget." Yes, the words were whimpered while my one hand massaged her, but it was the last part spoken that made me pause. Bitty wasn't ready for the physical *more* aspect of our relationship. It was the emotional that needed to be nurtured.

I would not hurt her by being a selfish asshole.

"Not like this." She tensed, her body going rigid in my arms. There was a small hiss of discomfort that escaped her lips while she attempted to push me away. I was having none of that, and with both hands wrapped around her midsection, I nestled her body against my own. "Bitty, stop. Listen to me before going off—"

"Is it because I look like shit?" Now that right there pissed me off. My cock had been hard—leaking against her back, fucking ready to find his home between her thighs.

"Don't." Thundering, my harsh tone made her stop her persistent attempt to pull herself out of my arms. "Turn around." My demand was met with defiance and a tiny sniff. And fuck me if my annoyance didn't evaporate in that instance. "Please, Maya. I need you to look at me."

Wiping her hand over her face, Bitty took a moment to compose herself and then turned to look at me. "What?"

"Enough." I gave a harsh nip to her bottom lip that caused her to whimper. "If I could fuck you right now, I would." Pressing up against her, I let her feel all of me. Natural reaction whenever she was near. I burned for her. "You feel that."

"Yes." A hiss. A goddamned plea for more was what I heard in that one word.

"Don't ever question my desire for you. You are all I see. All I need to be happy in this crazy, fucked-up world. You...you stubborn, hard-headed, beautiful woman, are my happiness."

"I'm sorry. It's just that I—"

"Understand."

At my interjection, she gave me a

timid smile and then turned back around. "Can you help me with my hair?"

Nothing else was said while I attended to her needs. Our bodies naked and wet, they brushed against the other. Reconnected with soft, innocent touches—enjoyed the feel of the other.

We needed that.

To just be.

For me, it was knowing that at that moment, she was safe. Healing. That her body and mind would get past this and I'd be there along the way, every step, because I loved her that damned much.

More than my own life.

"Hey, Miranda," I called out when I reached the nurses' station. "She's back in bed and starving. Is it okay for her to eat outside food? Maya's asking for homemade chicken noodle and a turkey club sandwich."

Laughing, she nodded. "Yeah, she's not on a special diet. And to be honest,

that sounds amazing right about now."
Subtle she was not.

"Are you hungry, Miranda?" I'd be more than happy to get her something too.

Blushing, she nodded and came to stand next to me. "I could eat."

Bumping my shoulder with hers, I smiled down at her. "You got it. Let me call it in and have one of our friends pick it up."

"Let me know what I owe—"

"My treat." She opened her mouth to argue, but I didn't let her. "Not up for discussion."

With that, I turned around and made my way back to Maya's room. We were still waiting for her doctor to come speak with her; I was ready to get her the fuck out of this place and back home. Feelings she shared with me.

I'd just turned the corner toward her room when I was stopped short. What I saw made every molecular cell in my body burn white hot. Anger consumed me. It was overwhelming. Hands shaking and body coiled tight, I rushed forward and grabbed their hand, pulling them back harshly without a care for their safety. I wanted blood.

A loud thud reverberated throughout the empty hallway, followed closely by a cry of pain. "Son of a bitch."

"What the fuck are you doing here?"

Now Available on Amazon
American Gangster
Tiffany Lordes

Buy Link

http://www.amazon.com/gp/produ
ct/B014K36ELQ

GAGE

"Fuck that pussy big boy and make me cum." Huh, little girl playing grown up. I let her talk her shit, while keeping up a nice slow stroke into her pussy. I was in no hurry to cum and she wasn't that good anyway.

She squeezed her overused pussy around my covered cock, fuck yeah I had my boy wrapped up, I wasn't about to fuck that without it.

I held her ass cheek in one hand and my nine in the other, that's how you roll in enemy territory. As much as she wasn't doing shit for me, her pussy never stopped cumming.

That's what eleven inches of pure hard steel will do to you. I was bored as fuck by the sixth or seventh time she came and pulled out and slipped into her ass. Not much better but it had a little tightness to it.

I off loaded and hopped off; took the condom off and headed for the bathroom while she shook and moaned all over the bed. Fuck this place, if this asshole thought he was going to catch me with this third-rate snatch and his big talk he was outta his fucking mind, this shit was small time, I didn't have time for this.

"Where's your boy?" I flushed the condom and watched it disappear before flushing again. She was still lolling around on the bed like she thought this was the Ritz and we were in love or some shit. "What's your rush baby, come back to bed."

"I would if there was something worth coming back to now where the fuck is he?" She looked hurt as fuck; yeah I care. I wasn't there when she decided to fuck her life down the drain with this shit I'm not responsible. I give a fuck.

She flounced off the bed and got into her clothes. At one point she was probably a nice looking chick, I guess that's why her owner had sent her. Too bad for him pussy didn't sway me; the shit was too easy to come by.

"He said I should bring you by when we were done." What the fuck? Who told this hump I needed to unwind as soon as I got into town? I like to get shit done and be out as soon as possible, preferably before the sun goes down.

The fact that he was procrastinating told me that he was up to no fucking good. If that was the case I hope he knew what the fuck he was doing. I'd come prepared for any contention, a man in my business better be on that shit if he wanted to survive.

I cleaned off my dick and shoved my shit back into my Trues. I wasn't dressed to impress, that's not my game, so it was jeans a tank and Tims.

I had my tats on full display and the stud in my ear was gleaming. I had the look down, no one would ever guess at the silver spoon background that had been wrenched away when daddy found younger pussy and left mommy and me high and dry. Motherfucking hump.

I couldn't be mad at the chick; she was just doing what she had to do to survive, same as me. Life had fucked me sideways when I wasn't looking and I was lived to pay that shit forward.

"Let's bounce, time's a wasting and I've got shit to do." She seemed nervous as fuck all of a sudden but I wasn't worried. I had a good idea what the fuck was up. Her boy had made certain promises and now couldn't come through. Same story different asshole!

Instead of manning the fuck up and coming clean, he had decided to make an end run around me it seemed like. Fine, we'll see how that shit plays.

I did a sweep of the area as soon as we hit the streets. Miss. Thing had picked me up at the airport and brought me directly to this place, which I'm guessing was two steps up from a flop.

The street wasn't the best but it wasn't the worse either. There were winos and junkies hanging around looking like rejects from a third world country instead of denizens of one of the major cities of the good ole U.S of fucking A.

She put a lot more wiggle in her ass than was necessary as she led me out to the car. I didn't have the heart to tell her that she was wasting her time, neither was I interested in making her feel good about herself.

I didn't see or feel any danger so I'm guessing the shit was supposed to go down at the next destination. I wondered on the way there how he was gonna play it. Would he come at me head on? Nah, if he had the balls he would've met me at the airport himself.

No he'd loosened me up with the pussy, next was probably some good Kush, most likely laced with some shit that it didn't need but was guaranteed to fuck me up.

Let me see, after I'm nice and fucked he'd make his play. He's probably gonna have a couple of his goons there to make himself look good.

Mind you, I'm the victim here; I'm the one who's been wronged. But none of that will matter as he justifies taking my life because he stole from me and couldn't repay.

The dumb fuck won't stop to ask himself why the fuck I would come all the way here alone. Why I hadn't brought not even one of my boys with me.

Hmm, either he thought I was real fucking stupid to believe his bullshit lies, or he was as fucking stupid as I had come to believe. I'm inclined to think it's the latter.

"So, how long are you planning to stay?" She lit a cigarette with a trembling hand as she looked around at anything but me. I guess it was hard to look at someone you were taking to their death.

I wonder how many men had had to suffer her washed up cunt before their demise, what a fucking insult. The least the fuck could do is find some better strange, the fuck, that's cold.

"Don't talk." The tone was stone cold, the face like marble. It was her first glimpse at the real me. Good let her get nervous, let her start to worry.

We pulled into a nice looking middle class community. I could tell the neighbors must hate this guy. Muscle cars parked up and down the street with muscle bound derelicts hanging out on the lawn while the houses on both sides of him looked like cookie cutter paradise.

There was the prerequisite pit bull and men in roped chains with their hats on backwards and their pants hanging off their ass. What a fucking stereotype.

When I get home I'm putting my foot in my second in command's ass. This asshole was his girl's cousin's cousin or some fuck and we were doing him a solid. That's what happens when you mix business with friendship, somebody always gets stupid.